A FIERY MATCH

RAFTER O RANCH BOOK TWO

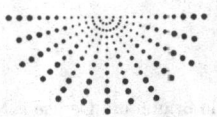

NATALIE BRIGHT
DENISE F. MCALLISTER

A Fiery Match
Paperback Edition
Copyright © 2022 Natalie Bright and Denise F. McAllister

CKN Christian Publishing
An Imprint of Wolfpack Publishing
5130 S. Fort Apache Rd. 215-380
Las Vegas, NV 89148

cknchristianpublishing.com

Print ISBN 978-1-63977-605-4
eBook ISBN 978-1-63977-303-9
LCCN 2022944126

A FIERY MATCH

"...For love is as strong as death, its jealousy as enduring as the grave. Love flashes like fire, the brightest kind of flame. Many waters cannot quench love, nor can rivers drown it..."

~Song of Solomon 8:6-7, New Living Translation

1
JANIE

JANIE OLSEN WATCHED THE VIVID COLORS OF the sunset reflected in her rear-view mirror. She drove east towards the next phase of her life. Driving to what, she did not know. Home was the Rafter O Ranch in the Texas Panhandle. The only thing was she never felt like she really belonged to the world of horses and cows, and she most certainly wouldn't fit in now.

Behind her was California and the military. Even after all night of driving, she still couldn't see a path clear to what was next. She had planned to get a motel room for the night, but her brain wouldn't shut off. Stopping for a quick coffee, a few stretches, jumping jacks and squats in the dark beside her car, and then she just kept driving.

It wasn't too late to re-up and consider making the military her career. As much as she loved it, she hesitated. Something was missing in her life. Where she might find it, or how to even know what the "it" might be was eluding her.

Home. It was the only place she could think of to go.

Janie and her four siblings were the fifth generation

of Olsens to live and work on the Rafter O Ranch lands. Her siblings had more interest in the ranch than Janie ever had. Other than the one time she got a wild hair and stepped onto the back of a bronc, riding and roping held no interest for her. And the little community of Dixon, Texas didn't offer much in the way of fulfilling career options for a girl for the rest of her life. She could do what most of the ones who stayed did—marry, have kids, become active in the PTA, the library friends, and volunteer at the county fair and stock shows. Only problem, the quiet, sedentary kind of life did not suit her.

And besides, she had never been on a date her entire life, so finding a husband was next to impossible. She was always one of the guys. Not exactly girlfriend material. Chasing after her two brothers, trying to be as good or better, and their friends counted her as one of the guys too. "Plain Jane" they had called her in high school.

"You're just too plain, and besides, you have the personality of a rock." This from the freshman trumpet player she had asked to prom in her junior year. If she couldn't get a freshman to go out with her, then it seemed she had no hope of ever dating anyone. So, she gave up on love and focused on her physical abilities and aspirations of joining the military.

Actually, Janie considered herself to be quite a fun person. And she loved traveling and thrived on physical challenges. Animals loved her, too. At this point in her life, she could live anywhere in the world, but nothing appealed to her. Either way, going back or moving forward, the future looked blank to her, and there wasn't a darn thing she could do about it. With a quick spin of the dial, Janie cranked up the radio and set her cruise control to eighty. The dashboard indicated an incoming call so she punched the answer button on the steering wheel.

"Janie. Where are you?"

"Hey, Mom. I'm just coming out of Albuquerque."

"You didn't stop for the night? Was that wise? You drive safe and we'll see you soon. I'll have a big breakfast waiting for you."

Her mother rapid-fired too many questions at her without a breath, so Janie just listened instead of offering details. "Be there as soon as I can."

"I hate that you missed Travis and Destynee's wedding. It was so beautiful. A little quirky but beautiful."

"Can't wait to hear all about it." Janie tapped her finger on the steering wheel as her mother continued over the next thirty minutes to report about her little brother's wedding to the local rodeo queen. The people and events she talked about seemed so foreign and a world away. They were all strangers to her now, and the bad thing was she wasn't all too sure she wanted them to be in her life again. Was that horrible?

At some mega convenience store on the interstate, Janie pulled in to stretch her legs and top off her tank. She perused the snack aisle but didn't get anything. Staying in shape was her number one priority and she did not want to wreck all the hard work she had invested in being lean and fit. One bag of chips would undo a week's worth of work. Chips were her absolute favorite, and she almost gave in but stayed strong and grabbed a bottle of water instead. Self-discipline was something she excelled at.

The lights of Amarillo hovered on the horizon, and she stayed on Interstate 40 and drove straight through the city without pulling over. Janie imagined her mother had been pacing the floor all night and would have the kitchen table piled with food. Tons of carbs, but she would make an exception since she had bypassed the snack earlier. She could almost taste the fluffy buttermilk biscuits and homemade plum jam, and it made her mouth water.

As she pulled out of Amarillo, the first hint of dawn illuminated the sky in front of her. The sun had not appeared on the horizon yet, but she knew it was there. Anticipation made her stomach clench. Seeing the family again, falling back into the old self she once was, made her dread the visit. The real person disappeared into the mousy Plain Jane of her existence. It almost made her turn around, but she had nothing to go back to. And nobody who cared.

She exited off the interstate and noted the brown grass instead of the green of spring on either side of the county road. They must have had a mild winter. With no snow and no spring rains, the treeless pasture remained sparse and brown. Still, the endless sky stretching for as far as she could see tugged at her heart. It was good to be almost home.

A trail of gray smoke rose, clearly visible in the predawn sky as she traveled from the washed-out low and topped the next rise. She gasped. It came from the direction of the Rafter O Ranch. Her stomach clenched, and her heart raced at the sight.

After several more miles, the smoke became denser and thicker. The road curved to cross a dry creek bed, and she turned off the pavement onto a dirt road that led to ranch headquarters. Following the road up a steep incline, the sight at the top made her stop the car.

Off to the distance, the ground was alive. The line between the horizon was bright orange, crimson red

4

flames chewing up the dry grass. Fuel to feed the unbeatable beast. It came from the direction of Rafter O headquarters, but from this far away, she couldn't tell if it was beyond or on this side of the main house. She punched the gas and headed towards the red sky.

As she watched the flames, she noticed that the smoke rose straight up, which was an indication that the breeze was minimal. She slowed at an intersection to allow a line of county firetrucks to pass and then turned to follow them.

2
MACK

FIRE CHIEF MACK GRIFFITT WATCHED, FROM the quiet of his Silverado pickup truck, the choking smoke of a range fire, clearly visible on the horizon. The pastures of the plains require fire to stay healthy, but this ocean of grass could fuel devastation like nothing else. Although his team of volunteers faced unbeatable odds, he had complete confidence in what they could achieve if they stayed on top of this burn. Behind him, the fire engines, tanker trucks, and pickups with trailers hauling dirt-moving equipment bounced and wormed their way along the dirt road. As they neared the fork, Mack pulled his pickup to one side, allowing the other vehicles to pass him by, one turning right and the other left. They would convene at a designated location in the middle of the pasture.

The slight breeze could grow into a stronger wind at any time and shift as more clouds rolled in with the rising sun. On the high plains, the wind was more of an enemy than the fire. He had reassigned all available men to this area. In addition to his Creek County Fire Department, several other teams from the surrounding towns had joined them. With the fire chief's coordinates and sectors divided, they had the fire almost fifty percent contained.

He knew his men were tired. They had been at it all night fighting the flames that had sparked from a single vehicle traveling on the blacktop that wound through the county. From what he could tell at the point it began, a chain must have been drug along the asphalt, igniting the weeds next to the road. Thank goodness other travelers had reported the flames within minutes after they had erupted.

Thankful for the first light of day, the next plan would be to start a back burn, but he hesitated because of the wind. Would it shift again? Either it would die down even more during the first hours of the dawn, or it would increase with a vengeance once the sun blazed full in the sky, and then they could lose all control.

The crew worked to unload the road graders from the trailers. He had assigned all available men to the tank trucks with water or blades, except for three volunteers who had stayed behind at the firehouse in Dixon. Only twice in his career did he have to contend with sending several crews in separate directions. He never wanted to feel that helpless again. It was a tough decision to make because he needed those men to relieve the others who had worked all night, but what if another call came in?

A text buzzed on his phone. He checked it and frowned.

HOW ARE YOU?

Christy. He glanced up to watch the men pull the trailers out of the way and start the equipment. He needed to get out there, so he decided to ignore her text. They had been dating almost a year, and she was a sweet, kind girl, also the president of the Chamber of Commerce. Sometimes he felt more like her first channel of information rather than a boyfriend. Her priority was to be in the know about everything and everyone. If he answered her text, she would never stop asking questions for the next thirty minutes. For as long as they had dated, she still had no clue about what his job entailed.

The volunteers had parked a few miles ahead of the fire front to scrape the grass and yucca in a wide swath on either side of the burn. From where his crew now parked, they would start a burn and control it as best they could. If the breeze, and it was just a breeze at this point, held from the same direction and did not shift on them, the back-burn would work.

As the sky grew lighter, he watched the smoke trails rise and curl several miles from their location. The grass was two to three feet in height because of a wet summer, which provided perfect conditions to fuel a hot and fast-moving fire. The direction of the drift of the smoke would give him a clue as to the exact path the burn would take. He needed to radio the county deputies so they could begin knocking on doors and evacuating people who might be in the path, if his back-burn plan did not work.

An unfamiliar car pulled through the wire gate behind his crew. He did not need any look-e-loos from the town right now, and couldn't afford someone getting hurt on his watch or getting in the way. The car parked, and before he could walk closer to see who the driver might be, one of the firemen called out. Mack stepped out of his truck, pausing to feel the wind on his face and determine the exact direction of the smoke.

"Boss. Is this where you want to start the burn? How far do you want us to spread out?"

Mack turned his attention to getting his crew situated, dismissing the text and the strange car. While the road graders scraped vegetation to clear a wide swath to create a fire break, he assigned one volunteer to handle the torch. The controlled burn would move against the wind, eating up the fuel at a slower rate. When the two burn paths meet, the dried grasses should all be used up, as long as conditions hold.

The volunteers got to work. Two men operated the drip torches, which would be used to ignite the back-burning fires. Others were standing by with shovels and rakes. They had unloaded two four-wheelers, each with reserve tanks of one hundred gallons of water. Dirt rose behind the maintainers as they cleared vegetation at a fast clip. He swirled his hand over his head to set the plan in motion, and it never hurt to say a prayer for everyone's safety.

He noticed a spitfire of a girl talking to one of his road grader drivers. She even climbed up onto the steps to talk to him in the cab and was giving him what for. Mack walked towards her and heard her say, "Get out! Just get out."

As he got closer, he noticed the petite brunette didn't have an ounce of fat on her body. Lean, with solid muscle, she exuded confidence and strength. It took him aback for a second, and he was almost cautious about approaching her. She looked like she could take him down in a split second, but he couldn't let some stranger ramrod his efforts. This was his fire scene, not hers.

He walked with purpose closer to her.

3
JANIE

JANIE FOLLOWED THE LINE OF FIRE ENGINES and pickup trucks. In the early morning light, she watched the men unload the trailers. Pulling through the wire gate, she recognized the Rafter O Ranch's maintainer grader. Her little brother Travis was at the wheel, a look of deep concentration on his face.

From behind her, another maintainer eased closer to her brother, but she did not recognize the driver. He seemed to be confused as to what direction he should go, first turning towards Travis, then making a circle and slowly chugging along in the opposite direction.

"Oh, good grief." Janie hopped out of the car and hurried over to the grader. He drove so slowly; in one fluid motion, she was able to jump onto the ladder and grab the handhold. She pounded on the window.

The driver stopped with a lurch, a look of surprise on his face.

"Get out," she yelled.

He looked at her with a blank stare.

"G...e...t... o...u...t..." She mouthed the words slowly so that he could read her lips.

"What are you doing?" a deep voice asked from behind her. She glanced over her shoulder. Even with her advantage on the ladder, she was only slightly taller than the mountain of a man who stood behind her. Dark hair curled at the top of his collar, and black eyes glinted mean from the most handsome face she had ever seen. The boy from high school had grown into a man. Her eyes were drawn to a neatly trimmed mustache and the Silverbelly hat balanced on his head. Her heart skipped a beat for a second.

"Why are you bothering my grader operator?"

She came back to reality. "He doesn't know what he's doing."

"Who are you?"

"Janie. Now ask him to get out so I can drive this piece of equipment and we can stop this fire."

"Ma'am, you need to leave. You have no authority to be ordering us around."

"Well, who died and left you in charge?" She pounded on the window again and gave the man inside her meanest look.

With a sheepish look on his face, the man inside the grader spun his chair around. Janie hopped to the ground so that he could swing the door open.

"Are you bringing us water and doughnuts?" the man asked as he shifted his bulk out of the seat and emerged from the cab.

"You need to get out and let me in," she answered, deciding to ignore the comment about doughnuts.

"You do not have the authority to drive a county vehicle." Again, the deep voice from behind her.

Janie ignored it, climbed into the driver's seat, and

pulled the door shut with a click. She looked out the front and could see her brother wearing a wide grin. He raised a hand in greeting. She replied with the same and adjusted the seat.

She glanced out the side window to see the angry firefighter glaring at her. She gave him a thumbs up and a big smile before engaging the gears and chugging away.

The delay had cost them as the smell of smoke seemed stronger now. She missed having her wild rag to tie over her face. She had a collection of various colors in a drawer in her old room. Not exactly Army-issue items that she could have taken with her. And her work gloves. She needed those too, but fretting would not get the job done, so she got to work.

Working together as a team, Janie knew the direction Travis would be going before he even turned that way. They had fought fires before, unfortunately. Her father had taught them well, and all of the Olsen kids were expected to pitch in when trouble came knocking. They never hesitated or questioned the situation, just faced it, prayed hard, and did what needed to be done. She had been riding in big equipment since she was little with her grandfather, and she felt he was with her now.

"Okay, Gramps. Let's see if we can get this fire contained." She dropped the blade to the ground.

The wind was on their side for the moment, and the smoke drifted away from them. She could see the flames about one hundred feet to her left as she kept scraping the grass and yucca, leaving a fuel-less path of dirt down one side of the burning field. The tanker trucks had moved closer to the line, wetting the ground as they went.

Time seemed to stand still. Janie focused on driving the maintainer, ignoring the intense thirst that made her mouth dry and her throat tickle. Plus, her stomach growled, making her think about the breakfast her mother was cooking. Janie couldn't send her a text about the delay because she had left her phone in her car.

Regardless of her physical issues, she kept driving, watching, and working alongside Travis until they made a huge swath on either side of the fire in the pasture at a diagonal.

A group of Rafter O cows huddled in the far corner of the pasture, and Janie wondered if she should cut the wire and drive them through but soon realized she didn't have any tools. But there was a gate somewhere along that fence. If she could locate it, maybe the cows would find it? She chided herself for not remembering her cell phone. That was a stupid move, and she blamed the distraction of that idiot oversized firefighter who had yelled at her. Why can't people just work together and be kind? She may be bossy, but she had good intentions.

Travis pulled to a stop and held up his cell phone. Janie shrugged her shoulders, pulled her piece of equipment to a stop and lifted up the blade, taking it out of gear before jumping to the ground and running over to Travis. He swung the door open.

She gave him a wide grin.

"Hello, little brother."

"Lose your cell phone?"

"Glad to see you too. Not lost, I left it in the car."

"I'm glad you're home, but we've got to get those cows out of that corner in case the wind shifts."

"I agree."

"If you can drive on down to the gate, I'll try to head them your way, but I'm not sure if they'll move without a man on horseback."

About that time, a tan pickup with the Rafter O brand

pulled close to them and her older brother Nathan hopped out and walked towards them.

"What are y'all standing around for? We don't have this thing contained yet. Let's get going. Hey, Janie."

No hug? It was good to know her family had missed her. "We're trying to figure out what to do with that bunch of cows. I don't have anything with me to cut the fence."

"I'll drive them with my truck. Travis, you can block them from taking off across the pasture. Janie, can you open the gate? If they're too scared, we'll just cut the wire and let them through."

And that's what they ended up doing, as Janie figured, and she jogged along the fence line to the gate. The smell of smoke was overwhelming so she covered her mouth with one arm as she ran. She waited by the gate and she could see Nathan trying to urge them along with no luck. Travis had hopped out of his maintainer and was waving his arms, but those cows wouldn't budge.

Janie eventually had to head back to her brothers just as Nathan finished cutting the last wire. They parked the maintainers at an angle to hem in the cows. She hopped to the ground and helped him peel back the fence, one wire at a time between cedar fence posts, to make a wide enough hole. The cows surged through without any coaxing.

"The good news is we have it close to seventy-five percent contained and we have five other fire departments on location. Mom is cooking food for the firefighters. They've been at it all night. We'll take a quick break and regroup."

Janie and Travis nodded their heads and then got back in their equipment, making tracks and scraping the ground for the slow return to ranch headquarters.

Just before Janie could turn and pass through the gate to get back on the road, a wild-eyed mustached man blocked her path. He stood, legs spread apart with arms crossed over his chest. Behind him stood the driver she had replaced.

She pulled to a stop and walked forward, ready to face the wrath that she probably deserved, but she'd never admit to.

"To answer your question from before, it was my father who died and left me in charge." With his chest thrust out, he stared her down with cold, dark eyes. "He was the fire chief for thirty-five years until he died in a fire trying to save someone. I took over, and that makes me in charge. I can assure you, Judy, that I am very capable of doing my job."

"That's not my name," she squeaked, which made her cheeks grow warm with embarrassment. She had never been intimidated by anyone or anything in her life. Without saying another word, she stomped to her car.

"I'm not done," he called out after her.

"Well, I am. And you're welcome. Glad to be of some help." She slammed the car door with a little extra muscle for effect and drove away without giving that annoying man another glance. She hoped her mother had kept the gravy warm.

4
JANIE

HOME. THE SMELLS OF FRESHLY BAKED BREAD and link sausages assaulted Janie's nose and brought a lump to her throat. Grace Olsen opened her arms wide, and Janie walked straight into them. She took a deep breath, recognizing the familiar perfume her mother always wore.

"I am so glad you're finally here. But you smell like smoke. Phew." Her mother backed up suddenly and wrinkled her nose.

"Happened to see the fire, so I stopped to help."

"Is it contained?"

"About seventy-five percent so, Nathan says. The guys are headed this way for a quick bite, and then we'll get back out there."

Their conversation was cut short as stomping boots of the Creek County Volunteer Fire Department descended upon the Rafter O Ranch headquarters, both from the front door and through the kitchen. Nathan stopped in the kitchen and pulled Janie into a warm hug.

"Hello, Sis."

"That's the hug I've been waiting for." She laughed. "Hey, Nathan. How are Indya and Gabriel? I'm looking forward to meeting that nephew of mine."

"Oh, he's a hoot. Has your energy and quick wit." Nathan's face beamed with pride.

"And, Indya? Mom said y'all opened an art gallery in Amarillo."

"Yeah, you should come see it sometime. We're thinking about building a house."

"I want to see some of your artwork. Mom told me about your gallery and Travis's wedding. Seems like I've missed so much. And how is Libbie doing?" The sister between her and the youngest, Travis. Their lives seemed so far apart from her world.

"Libbie is all about college and her friends." Grace smiled. "Your father keeps telling me to give her some space."

As the firefighters helped themselves to coffee, Grace grabbed platters of sausages and pancakes and headed towards the dining room. Janie hurried up the back staircase to wash her hands and face. She would unload her car later.

Her old room seemed familiar but different. Or maybe she was the one who had changed. No longer the timid girl who stood in the back, out of the way. The military had given her confidence, and she had learned things she never thought possible, and traveled a bit too. This room had belonged to her child-self. Now she had outgrown it and her hometown too. But there was no place else to go. No one was waiting for her.

By the time she made it downstairs, there wasn't a seat left at the dining room table. She eased around to the sideboard and filled her plate, passing behind the fire chief who sat in the middle on one side. Conversation

17

was absent as the men focused on their plates of food. Surprised that he—she didn't even know his name—wasn't sitting at the head telling everyone when they could take a bite. Janie was used to strong, arrogant men after serving in the military, but this guy was beyond and out of line.

She took her plate into the kitchen and sat at the bar. Closing her eyes and savoring every bite of the carb-laden biscuits and gravy. Heaven in her mouth.

A giggle from her mother made her eyes open, and a warm hand caressed her shoulder.

"You missed my cooking, didn't you?"

"Yes, Mom, I did." Janie responded with a laugh. Still consciously aware of the man in charge, she had to learn more. "Do you know the fire chief?"

"Yes, Jim's boy. You remember Jim Griffitt, don't you? He was fire chief for years and years, served on the city council, and even ran for mayor before he took over the fire department."

Janie shook her head. "I don't recall him." But she remembered his son, Mack, all too well.

"He died in a fire trying to rescue some kids. His son, Mack, grew up in the firehouse. He dropped out of college, came back to Dixon to take over after his father passed. Seemed only right that he would get the job."

Janie stood to refill her coffee cup. "Has their family lived here as long as we have?"

"Funny you should ask because actually, the Griffitts were one of the first settlers in this area as well. It was your great-great-grandfather who donated the land. There was some kind of feud between the two families, but I'm not sure what it was about. Lost in time, I guess. My aunt told me it had something to do with your great-great-grandmother." Her mother winked.

"That's interesting. The chief seems to be very driven and grouchy. I thought he was going to punch me out there." Janie shook her head.

"If you're talking about me, then yes. I take my job very seriously." A deep voice suddenly filled the kitchen from behind her. "Grace, it was delicious. Thanks for feeding my men and me." Grace Olsen snickered as she looked from Mack to Janie. "Anytime, Mack. Thanks for your work." She picked up another platter of pancakes, disappearing into the dining room. Janie turned on the bar stool and stared at the man who stood behind her with the attitude.

"I was just trying to help. I do know how to operate equipment."

"Well, you can help by staying out of the way and allowing my trained firefighters to do their job."

"I am just as capable as they are."

"Says who? I have no idea who you are."

"Says me!" Of all the places this infuriating man could be on the planet, she had to deal with this kind of arrogance in her own home.

Ignoring her last comment, Mack put his empty plate into the sink and turned to join his men again.

"What's next, Chief?" one of the men asked.

Janie remained in the kitchen, fuming. She could hear the discussion, interrupted every so often by a deeper voice that irritated her and intrigued her at the same time. Her pride did not allow her to join the others in the dining room.

But she wasn't remaining in the house, that's for sure. She'd be out there fighting alongside the volunteers despite that arrogant beast.

With a few calls to Grace in thanks for the meal, the men suddenly left as quickly as they had arrived. Janie grabbed her little brother's arm before he made it out the back door.

"So, what's the plan?" she asked.

"I'm going to cut a fire break along our west fence line. If the wind shifts, our headquarters is done for," Travis said. "The other guys are going to relieve the men tending to the backburn, and give them a chance to eat. Mom's making more pancakes, that's what I heard her say."

"Great. I'm taking our backhoe and following you."

"I think the fire is about to play out, as long as the wind holds." Travis put on his gloves with Janie close behind. She grabbed a spare pair of gloves from a drawer in the mud room. Hopefully that unbearable fire chief would be on the other side of the county.

"Hold up, dear sister." Janie felt her younger sister's hand on her shoulder. "Glad you're back home, but I need your help."

Janie turned. "Hey, Sis. What are we doing?"

"Saddling up and moving the horses closer to head-quarters, just in case this fire gets out of hand." Angie walked ahead. "And don't forget to change your boots."

She looked at her feet, not even thinking about the biker boots she wore. "No, ma'am. You know I don't do horses. I have a big yellow piece of machinery with my name on it."

"I need you, otherwise I wouldn't ask. Travis is part of the volunteer fire department now, and I can't find Dad. Mom! Where's Dad?"

Grace was too busy mixing up more pancake batter to answer, so Angie looked at Janie with pleading eyes. "It'll only take a few minutes. I promise."

Janie couldn't say no to that look. She had failed many times before.

5
JANIE

THE RAFTER O RANCH KEPT ABOUT TWENTY horses in the north pasture. Some were ones that Travis had started training as colts, a few belonged to ranch hands, and some were in training. Only a handful of horses stayed in the barn, ones that Travis was training for clients. The smell of smoke permeated the barn as well. Janie cleared her throat.

"Grab that gray one, Janie. She's gentle. You do remember how to saddle a horse, don't ya?"

Janie smirked and rolled her eyes. "Yes, I remember how to saddle a horse. It's just the riding part I'm not too crazy about. Remember that time I nearly got decapitated by that tree branch when my horse took off with me?"

She led the horse into the wash rack and hooked up her halter to the crosstie chains attached to the wall. She grabbed a saddle blanket and saddle while the horse stood quietly, as she was supposed to.

"You'll be fine. Don't let that childhood memory mess with you. That was nearly twenty years ago." Angie tied her horse to a stall's bars and was quickly tacked up. "We just need to steer the pasture horses up into the corral close to headquarters. That way, we can keep an eye on them as we monitor the fire. I'll tell you what to do. Piece of cake. No worries."

Easy for you to say. Janie's eyebrows went up and down. Her sister was the real rancher and had pretty much taken over when their father had a health scare and older brother, Nathan, became an artist and got married.

Ranching was never really her thing, even though their father had taught all the kids the basics about horses, cows, and the land. What was her thing, exactly? And what was she going to do with her life now that she was out of the military? At this moment, she had to focus on the job at hand—the fire. So, she would follow Angie's lead.

She sat on a stool and pulled on Angie's boots. They were the same size. After her horse was tacked up, she led it into the barn's hallway and, after two tries, hoisted herself up into the saddle. Angie was already out the door. She was giving instructions to a ranch hand who stood at the barn opening.

"Wait up, Ang!"

"C'mon, slowpoke," her sister answered. "We need to get a move on. The fire's not waitin' on us."

Janie nudged her horse into a trot to catch up. "What's this horse's name?"

"Who cares? Call her 'Gray' if you need a name."

Janie mumbled to herself. Well, I just might need to know her name when I go flying in the air as she bucks me off. "You won't do that, will you, girl?"

The horse's ears twitched back and forth as though listening and Janie patted her neck.

Angie glanced back at her. "Don't pamper her. This ain't no leisurely trail ride on a dude ranch. We've got work to do. The horses will be nervous with the smell of smoke in the air. Are you up for it?"

Janie scowled. "Yes. Let's just get it done. Tell me what to do."

"Loosen your rein a little. Don't put a death grip on her mouth, or you'll worry her. We don't need that around a herd of horses we're trying to round up. Keep up with me. Put her into a lope. There's the herd up there. We'll stay together and go around to the right. When I tell you, if I see a few separating to go their own way, I'll holler for you to get behind and steer them towards home. Can you do that?"

"Yes, ma'am." Janie considered saluting but decided against it. Angie could be touchy at times. Best to just listen and follow orders.

Both girls rode their horses at a medium lope behind the remuda. Suddenly Angie picked up the pace and, at a faster gallop, turned the group back towards head-quarters.

"Janie!" she yelled. "Get around to the left. Hurry! They're starting to break away."

"C'mon, Gray. Don't make me look like a jerk." Janie made kissy and "Hah!" sounds to the mare, anything to kick her into the next gear. Luckily, the horse complied.

The almost-renegade horses on Janie's side got in sync with the group and Angie yelled again. "Janie! Stay towards the back. I'll lead them to the corral. One of the ranch hands will keep the gate open for us."

Janie was sweating and her adrenaline raced as the thundering hooves pressed on around them, becoming one entity snaking through the corral opening. When all the horses were in, jockeying for their own positions, some biting and bucking, the ranch hand latched the gate.

Angie steered her horse next to Janie's and gave her a high five. "Good job, Sis. See, you are a cowgirl after all."

"I don't know about that. But we got the job done." She had to smile a little to herself. And she couldn't resist giving Gray a pat on her neck when Angie was looking the other way.

The sisters sat their horses and watched the herd settling down in the corral. Janie was catching her own breath and looked to the sky to their right. "Looks like the smoke trail is dying down. Maybe they've got the fire under control now."

"Sure hope so." Angie reined her horse towards the barn. "Let's brush these guys off and turn them out."

Janie followed. She was glad she was able to help Angie and that nothing bad had happened. But it was something she didn't want to do every day. How Angie loved it so much was a mystery to her.

Inside the barn, Angie had already tied her horse to a stall and was lifting the saddle down to put it on a rack. "You did good, Janie. Hope that helps you forget your childhood mishap with horses."

Janie was listening as she readied to dismount, raising her right leg over the horse... when her left foot got hung in the stirrup and she bobbled, grabbing for the horse's mane, anything to stabilize herself. But before she knew it, she was flat on her back on the ground with a thud. Gray glanced sideways at her.

"Owwwww..." She didn't move for a few seconds.

"Are you okay, Janie? What in the world happened?"

Janie sat up while holding the back of her head and rubbing her hip.

"I'm fine." She wouldn't tell Angie she saw a few stars floating in front of her eyes.

Angie stifled a chuckle. "At least you didn't do that when we were rounding up the herd. No one ever called you graceful growing up."

"Shut up. And don't tell Mom. Now, let's go find Travis and Nathan and see if they need any help."

And, hopefully, avoid that infuriating man.

6

JANIE

"Janie, I volunteered you to help the mayor."

Janie sighed. Her mother couldn't stand for people to be idle around the house for very long. With the fire contained in the early evening, the Olsen siblings had driven along the edges of the burned ground with shovels, putting out hotspots and worrying over smoldering yucca. The fire had only crept onto one edge of the Rafter O, taking almost fifty acres. Janie had slept later than usual after collapsing onto her old mattress last night. She had really missed that bed.

"Good morning, Mother." She tried to hide the irritation in her voice. A job. Really?

She slumped onto the barstool. Her mom placed a mug with the Rafter O brand on one side in front of her. Janie had to pause and appreciate the smell of fresh ground coffee beans and the resulting liquid. "Thanks. This is all I need because I might go running later. I can't run after a heavy meal."

Ignoring her comments, a plate with two poached

eggs, a slab of ham, and a buttery biscuit appeared before her.

"Nonsense. You are as skinny as a beanpole. Eat up." Her mother turned to get her own mug of coffee and sat down next to her.

"Got any sand plum jam left?" Janie sighed. No sense in arguing, and her mother's homemade jam made everything in the world seem right. "I promised Dad I would look at the John Deere and change the oil. What else does he need me to do?"

"I'm sure your father is glad to have you back, but the county mechanic's wife is having a terrible time with her pregnancy and is due within the next few weeks. Jim needs to be home with his wife, and I told Mayor Blake that you could fill in until he gets back from paternity leave."

Great. "If I hang around here much longer, you'll have me a full-time job and signed up for a 601K plan," mumbled Janie. "And sacking groceries in my spare time."

"It's 501K, and I heard that."

Janie rolled her eyes. "I'm happy to help around here until Dad feels better. I don't mind ranch work."

Her father was still recovering from an angina attack. They were all struggling with his health issues, but none more than her dad. She could sense his frustration the moment she arrived home. He had never been one to sit around the house.

No matter how old she got or how many experiences she had, traveling all over the world, for gosh sakes, her mother could still make her feel like she was thirteen. Her mother always told her she was the challenging child because she had no direction. Apparently, old habits die hard, and her mom still felt the need to steer her life.

"Okay, sure, Mom. Tell the mayor I'll be glad to help out. When does he want me there?"

"Oh great, I'll give him a call. Thanks, dear. I'll make you your favorite for dinner. Enchilada casserole."

Janie smiled in between bites of the biscuit piled high with jam. There were some perks to keeping peace with her mother, her cooking being one of them.

Mrs. Olsen disappeared down the hallway. "I'll make that lemon pound cake you like so much for dessert."

Janie laughed loudly. "Thanks, Mom!"

Grace Olsen was one of the women Janie admired most. Totally committed to her family and the Rafter O, Grace did everything she could to make everyone else's life easier. She was the ultimate rancher's wife. No question that her mom and dad were a team. Life in small-town America held no appeal for Janie. What in the world did her mother do all day? Cooking, cleaning, running errands for her father, and serving on every committee that needed a warm body with the same people day after day.

Janie wanted to travel and have a higher purpose than running a household. The truth was she wasn't even sure if she wanted kids, and she would probably be cast out of town for saying so. That's what you did in Dixon, Texas. Graduate high school, maybe go off to college, but for sure come back home at some point to raise a family and be a model citizen of service to your community. No thanks.

During her time with the military, Janie had been sent to Japan and Germany, and she thoroughly enjoyed seeing how different parts of the world lived. She ate rice cakes and purple ice cream in Japan but drew the line at insects and horse meat. In Germany she liked bratwurst and schnitzel and pretzels. She also gained five pounds there, although she was constantly exercising.

Coming back to her small Texas hometown made it seem... small... and limiting, no potential. She wanted to see more of the world, to be thrilled by life's experiences, not settle for what was expected of her.

She had also learned everything there was to know about engines and motor parts, on automobiles and trucks mainly but also some aspects of aircraft maintenance. Her fellow enlistees welcomed her into their fold... after some initial hiccups due to her gender, but after that was out of the way, they admired her precision, attention to detail, and knack for being a fast learner and having a near-photographic memory when the supervisor taught a procedure. Many of the guys asked for her help. She had always had a knack for keeping the ranch equipment tuned up and running, something she had learned from her grandfather and father. Out of necessity, rural families were self-sufficient. If you wanted it to work, you had to learn how to fix it.

Plain Jane didn't exist in the military environment since the men were not comparing her to a beauty queen or someone they might date. They respected her for her intelligence. And she thrived. Actually, missed it. She almost felt like a star in the service, popular even.

Here she was, back to being Plain Jane since walking back into her childhood bedroom. And the only expectations the town and her family had for her were to get married and have babies.

So now her mother had gotten her a job. Always pondering what was next for her life, Janie decided to do the job for however long, while she was making up her mind about where she was headed, where to live, and what kind of work would fulfill her.

Maybe she'd contact the Army again, maybe re-up. Travel the world on their dime. Or apply for jobs with motors and mechanical parts. She didn't mind getting dirty.

What she did mind was being stuck. In a place with no future.

7

JANIE

On Monday morning, Janie arrived at the Creek County barn precisely at eight o'clock to find one of the sheriff's deputies waiting on her. She realized she had no keys, but one of the overhead doors was already open.

Located on the edge of town, just a few blocks from the fire station, the large Quonset barn housed the tractors, mowers, and tools that belonged to the city and county.

"Where's Jim? He usually gets here at seven," the man asked.

"I'm filling in for him for a while. What can I help you with?"

She took a second glance, and then it turned awkward. Now a deputy, she remembered this guy, Jack Skinner, with full clarity. His brother had been the one who told her she had no personality when they were kids. The skinny kid with braces had turned into a slender, handsome man with the same tousled blonde hair. But then, just about every man looked good in a uniform.

"Do you remember me from school?" he asked.

"Of course," she laughed. "There weren't that many in our school."

"You asked my little brother out once."

Janie's cheeks blushed. "Yes, I did. To the prom."

"He turned you down. I remember. What happened to you after that?"

"I graduated, and after working in the city, I joined the military."

"Really?"

More awkward silence. She had already asked him once if he needed help with something, so she saw no need to ask again. Hanging on a peg by the glass-fronted office was a pair of gray overalls. She tugged them down and stepped one leg at a time without taking her shoes off and zipped them up. A little long in the legs, but they'd work fine.

"I need my cruiser tuned up a bit, but it can wait until Big Jim gets back, I guess."

"Suit yourself." Janie turned with a shrug and began exploring the shop, learning how the tools and equipment were arranged.

Deputy Skinner cleared his throat. "A bunch of us meet for pizza and beer at Marcella's. You should join us. We could talk about old times. Nothing fancy. How about tonight? Just meet me there. What you're wearing is fine."

She was shocked when all that came tumbling out of his mouth. He said it like she didn't own anything other than overalls, and she didn't want to talk about old times, that was for certain. She was trying to forget her awkward years.

"I'm not in town for long."

"Is that so? Well, if you change your mind, it's just over the county line."

"Yes, I know where it is."

"You might as well check out my ride while I'm here."

Despite the fact that she hadn't even been to the city office to fill out employment paperwork, it didn't deter her. Might as well get started. She sure hoped she was getting paid. Forgot to ask her mother about that. No telling what the deal might have been that her mom made.

The cruiser had a loose hose, and she refilled the windshield wiper fluid, and with that easy fix, he was out the door in no time. She really should get over to the city human resources department. Before she could get the grease off her hands, the mayor walked in and called out a hello.

"You must be Janie." He stretched out his hand and she shook it. "I brought you the keys."

For a small-town mayor, Janie had never seen him when he wasn't in his mayoral gear—dressed to the nines in a dark tailored suit, white shirt, and red tie, Mayor Blake was always in politicking mode with a smile that revealed perfect teeth and a booming voice. It was a bit much for the small town of Dixon, making Janie wonder if he had higher aspirations. He had been mayor for as long as she could remember.

"I called your mom as soon as I heard you were back in town. I know that you kept all of the Rafter O equipment in tip-top shape. Your father always used to say, 'I'll have Janie take a look at it.'" He followed that with a deep belly laugh. "We really appreciate your helping us out at the county barn for a while."

"How is Jim's wife doing?"

"She hasn't delivered yet, but he's taking her to Amarillo today so they can monitor her."

They chatted for several minutes.

"I'll check on you again later."

She waved goodbye and turned to look around the shop. Could use some organizing. An outline of every tool was drawn on the peg board, but there wasn't a tool to be found anywhere near the tool bench or on the board. She began gathering up the tools from various locations in the shop and putting them in their proper place.

The morning passed by fast without any more visitors. She ate her lunch, a ham sandwich and a banana, downed a bottle of water, and then got back to it. It was quiet on the edge of town, and sitting at the entrance of the shop, she had a view across the grass to the blacktop that wound through an endless stretch of pasture grass.

After looking around the shop, she decided to sharpen the mower blades. Even though the grass was a dull brown now, they'd need the mower in top condition as soon as it greened up and the rains came. No reason to put it off, and it would make the afternoon pass by faster.

She smiled to herself as thoughts of her time with the Army paraded across her mind. In the beginning, marching really annoyed her. Basic training had been more difficult than she ever imagined, but eventually, she liked the discipline of everything. She learned how to pack and polish and keep everything in its place. If truth be known, she had already learned some of that from her father, who was a stickler for doing things right, at least in his opinion of right.

It was somewhat of a challenge being a woman in the service. Ultimately, while working together and depending on every member of the team, they all developed a genuine respect for one another. But she wondered where they were now. A few of the guys in her unit had reenlisted, but she hadn't heard a word, text, or email, nothing. It was as if that part of her life never existed, or as if she lived in two separate worlds. She couldn't decide if she liked being back here in her hometown.

So typical that no one in this town would ever see her as anything more than "Plain Jane", the new county mechanic. Pathetic.

Why couldn't she for once be the girl in the slinky dress that turns every head in the room? It just wasn't in her stars. She might as well face it. The image of a certain fire chief passed through her mind, and for some reason, being a Plain Jane bothered her even more.

8
MACK / JANIE

MACK COULDN'T SEE THE COUNTY'S MECHANIC, Jim, but he heard the clank of a wrench from beneath the tractor.

"Hey, Big Jim. If you have time, one of our water tankers has a grind. Might be the starter."

He could see steel-toed work boots sticking out from behind the oversized back tractor tire. He'd never noticed how tiny Big Jim's feet were.

"No hurry on that tanker, but I would appreciate it if you could get to it right away."

The squeak of wheels resulted in the dolly rolling out a girl with a grease-smudged face who was wielding a wrench. Her gloves looked to be about two sizes too big. A shine of surprise grazed her eyes, and then it vanished quickly.

She gave him an annoyed look and wheeled back under the tractor.

"Busy."

He immediately recognized the bossy girl who had interrupted his grass-fire scene. What was she doing in

Dixon, and what had he done to deserve this aggravation? "Where's Big Jim?"

"Having a baby."

"Why are *you* here?"

"Just hanging out, I guess." There was humor in her voice, but he didn't feel like laughing.

"Seriously, what are you doing here?"

"I'm helping out. I will get to your tanker when I can."

"It's the middle of fall. There isn't anything that needs mowing now, so you can stop what you're doing and look at my tanker. We have to keep the fire equipment in working order."

"I'm running the shop now and I can prioritize the work as I see appropriate." That last one was stretching the truth, but it sounded impressive, so she was going with it. Actually, she really wasn't sure where her authority started and ended. She didn't even know if she'd be getting paid for this job.

"Does the mayor know you're in here?"

"Of course. Does he know *you're* here?"

"I need you to clear this out of the way so I can pull in the fire department truck."

His beeper buzzed, and he flipped open his phone.

"Yes. I can," he spoke into his silver cellphone. "Tell her I'll be right there."

Janie rolled out from under the tractor again.

"Gotta go." He turned and left.

She gave him a salute and a smirk which he saw when he suddenly turned around.

"Name's Mack. I don't believe I caught yours."

"Janie."

Her heart would not slow down no matter how many deep breaths she took. The sight of the fire chief standing there, looking down at her, made her legs feel like jelly. Dang that man. He was even better looking all cleaned up, without smoke on his face and black soot on his clothes. He had worn his official chief's uniform, dark blue pants, starched white shirt, gold badge.

Obviously, a man not too savvy with the next generation of electronics. Who still carried a flip phone, for gosh sakes?

~

HER PHONE BUZZED. Pulling a glove off first, she dug into her pocket.

"Janie, it's your mother."

"Yes, Mom, I know it's you."

"Would you please run over to Miss Hattie's and pick up my casserole dish? She saved it for me from the book club meeting."

"Sure, Mom. No problem. Text me the address." Janie interrupted her mother because she didn't want a rundown about their once-a-month rummy get-together. That conversation could go on for another thirty minutes.

Not sure what needed locking up as she walked around the shop, she closed cabinets, shut drawers, and pulled down the two overhead doors, latching the inside lock. Light switches flipped off, and she locked the door behind her.

~

AS SHE ARRIVED at Miss Hattie's house, she noticed the fire chief's truck parked out front and she heard voices coming from the backyard.

38

Walking through the arbor to the side of the house, she found Mack waving a broom at the pecan tree that covered most of the tiny backyard. Miss Hattie was standing next to him wearing pink yoga pants, a lime green top, and a faded flower sack apron that she had worn as long as Janie could remember.

"Come on, Sweety. Sweety, get down this instant." Miss Hattie's wrinkled face was turned into a deep frown and tears pooled in her eyes.

Mack was poking the broom at the branch beneath where a black and white tabby sat and stared down from her perch, seemingly without a care in the world.

"Oh, Janie, you're here. Good. I'll get that dish for you in just a minute. I can't get Sweety out of the tree."

Mack gave her a glance but no greeting. She didn't acknowledge him either. She watched him jab the broom and listened to Miss Hattie's pleas in a sing-songy voice until she could not stand it any longer.

"You're just scaring her." Janie moved up beside him and snatched the broom from his hand. "Get out of the way."

"Oh, you think you can do any better?"

"I know I can." She threw the broom aside and held out her arms. "Sweety. Come on. Your mama is worried about you. Get down from that tree."

Sweety's ears perked as she watched Janie, and then she stood and cautiously moved one front paw and then another. Suddenly, in a flash, she jumped from one branch to the next and landed in Janie's arms, purring to beat the band.

"She's down," Miss Hattie buried her face in the cat's back and sobbed. "Oh my. Thank you. Thank you, Janie."

Mack bent to pick up the broom and they all followed Miss Hattie to her back door.

"You both must come in and have a piece of coconut pie. I just took it out of the oven. And I can make some coffee right quick."

"No thanks, ma'am. I need to get going. I just need the casserole dish."

"You can't stay for a minute and eat pie? You too good for us?" Mack's tone was rough.

She looked at him in surprise. What was with all the animosity?

"And have you looked at that tanker yet?"

"No, I just got off work." Janie handed the cat over to its owner. "And, not that it's any of your business, but I, uh, have a date. I can't stay."

Miss Hattie watched their exchange with a silly grin on her face, her eyes glued to Mack and then to Janie, and then back to Mack.

Janie dreaded the whole thing because she knew the Dixon gossip mill would go nuts after this.

"A date?" He looked at her with the most incredulous expression on his face, part surprise and part horror.

That old familiar hurt hit her gut. The one where no one could ever imagine a guy in his right mind would want to ask Plain Jane out. She pushed down the hurt and covered it with her usual rough exterior.

"You don't think anyone in this town would ask me out?"

"That's not what I meant."

She stepped inside Miss Hattie's back door and grabbed the dish that was on the table.

Janie came back outside and stopped on the top steps. From that vantage point, she could look Mack directly in the eyes. "I'll have you know that I've had plenty of offers."

"Offers for what?" one corner of his mouth turned up in a half-grin. He was teasing her now.

"Never mind." Her blood boiled. That was the most infuriating man she'd ever known in her life.

She slammed the door to her car, still fuming. A beer sounded good right about now.

9

JANIE

JUST OVER THE COUNTY LINE, NESTLED IN among a grove of cottonwood trees, was the pizza joint. The lot was encircled with towering evergreens, which explained why the place wasn't visible from the highway unless you knew where to turn.

Janie only realized her mistake at the exact moment she walked into Marcella's. Country music blasted her ears, but the place held all of the usual atmospheres of a good pizza place, although eclectic. Wooden floors, deer heads on the walls, and an impressive neon light collection. Of course, obligatory for the Italian theme, were the red and white checkered plastic tablecloths.

She should have at least cleaned her face and brushed her hair. Instead, she had on a plain T-shirt, the same jeans that she had worn underneath the overalls all day, and still had on her work boots which clomped against the wooden floor. Deputy Jack waved a hand from a back table. A few women from the city office looked familiar, probably went to high school with them, and several of the city maintenance crew gave her a nod. Before heading that way, she slipped into the women's restroom to survey the disaster that was her appearance. Her cheeks were still flushed with anger from the encounter with the fire chief, and her hair was plastered flat on her head from the ball cap she had worn all day. Bending over, head upside down, she ran her hands through her hair to fluff it up. When she came up and looked in the mirror, she noticed the grease smudge.

Grabbing a paper towel, she scrubbed her cheek until it glowed red as though somebody had back-handed her. But she did have some tinted lip gloss in her pocket. That would have to do. Tucking in her T-shirt and then untucking it, she gave a big sigh and walked out of the ladies' room.

Deputy Jack waved again as she emerged. Might as well get this over with. She could be friendly, besides, she needed to figure out how to get on the county payroll. The mayor hadn't exactly said how many weeks she'd be working.

Janie squinted her eyes against the glaring neon sign that read *Marcella's*, which occupied the entire space behind the bar. Still aggravated at herself and constantly self-conscious about her looks, she walked slowly towards the back table. Her hair had always been thin, dull, brown locks that settled lifelessly on her shoulders. As opposed to her sister Angie, whose blonde hair was always perfectly in place and shiny with curls. Her youngest sister, Libbie, had been a cheerleader, and of course, everyone knew her. Janie had given up long ago with trying to outshine her sisters. It is what it is, she always told herself. Wishing wouldn't make it any different.

She had time for one beer, maybe a slice or two, and then home to bed. She wanted to get to the shop early the next day and do some more cleaning and reorganizing. She had noticed a stack of tools and boxes of parts underneath a metal workbench and wanted to find places for each of them.

Driven by a parched thirst for something cold rather than the company of new friends, she headed towards the back table and sat down beside the deputy. He gave her a big toothy grin.

"What're ya havin' this fine evening?"

Funny how she hadn't noticed him that much in the glare of the fluorescent lights this morning at the county barn, but he was kind of cute in a small-town, boy-next-door sort of way. Definitely older than her. Those unruly blonde curls grazed his shirt collar, and his confidence was attractive. He turned green eyes her way, raising an eyebrow.

She willed herself not to stare and blinked. "Just a beer. Cold."

"You're at the right place. I'll be back in a minute."

That was very gentlemanly and surprising. He could've simply waved for a waitress. Instead, he was back in a few seconds and plopped a bottle in front of her, ice and condensation running down the side. She picked it up and took a deep chug.

"Thank you." Janie swallowed another swig.

He laughed. "Was your day that bad?"

She gulped another drink and then remembered there were other people at the table. Looking up, she smiled shyly.

"This is Janie, everybody. She'll be helping out at the county barn." He continued to name everyone at the table, which she ignored. She would never know any of these people, and would probably never be back here again. One beer, and she would be going home anyway.

"Has Jim's wife had their baby?"

"I'm not sure. Today was my first day at the shop."

"You're a mechanic?"

"Yes, I just finished a stint in the military, and believe it or not, that's where my talent lies."

"I don't remember you from high school."

"She asked my brother out when he was a freshman." Deputy Jack grinned.

"You don't look familiar at all. I'm sorry."

Janie didn't offer any personal information, and no one connected her to the Rafter O Ranch or to her more popular brothers and sisters. She drank her beer in silence and listened to the friendly banter between people who had obviously worked together for many years. And they had known each other's families for many years before that.

"If you're working at the county barn, you need to come see me. I'm on the second floor of the courthouse, and we'll get you on the payroll," one of the girls said.

"Oh, yes. Thank you! The mayor wasn't specific about what I should do."

"Yes, he did mention you to me. So come by first thing tomorrow, and we'll get you fixed up."

That was worth her taking time to join the group. The waitress appeared and asked if she needed another, but she had a few swigs left and then she would be gone, so she shook her head, no, followed by "Thanks."

The waitress was back within a few more minutes with two extra-large pizza pies, which she placed at either end of the long table. Pepperoni and cheese aroma filled Janie's nose, making her stomach growl.

"Help yourself." Jack casually laid an arm on the back of her chair.

Janie reached for a plate and picked out a slice.

"Oh, here's Mack," one of the girls at the table said with bright eyes and a big smile. "Let's make room."

Chairs screeched on cement floors as everyone made space for him. Janie hunkered over her pizza slice, trying to figure out how to escape. Mack. The fire chief. There could only be one Mack in this town.

Too late. He pulled out a chair for a blonde, and as he looked up, his eyes met Janie's. His eyebrows arched in surprise as he looked from Janie to the deputy and then back again.

Janie gave him a half-smile. Almost caught in a lie. They could be on a date, after all, they were sitting next to each other. It was none of his business anyway what this was. Although, when Mack looked her way, the deputy casually put his arm around her. Good move, deputy, although it was all she could do to keep from cringing. She hadn't expected that sudden touch. She didn't want anything new to deal with because there would be hurt feelings, and she'd have to unleash her mean side.

"Hi, I'm Christy. I work at the Dixon Chamber of Commerce," the blonde bubbled.

"I'm Janie. We went to high school together."

"The new mechanic at the county barn." Christy stated the obvious with information everyone already knew. "We went to high school together?"

"Yes, we did."

"I just don't remember you. Has Jim's wife had their baby yet?"

And so proceeded the same conversation that had occurred half an hour before to bring Christy up-to-speed on what everyone knew about Jim becoming a dad. Janie rolled her eyes. For the next round, she ordered iced tea, took a sip, and caught the glance of Mack over the glass, who held a half-grin and humor sparkling in his eyes.

She downed the iced tea in record time as her eyes drifted to watch Mack, who seemed to be completely enthralled in whatever Chamber Christy was saying.

Janie stood. "It was really nice meeting you all. I have an early morning tomorrow."

"See you tomorrow," the deputy said.

"Thanks for inviting me." She returned his smile.

"I'll walk you out. I need to ask you about that repair on the tanker." To her surprise, Mack stood and followed her outside.

She didn't stop walking until she was next to her car. She calmly looked up at the fire chief, although her heart was thumping out of her chest. On the inside, she was far from at ease.

10

JANIE

"WAS THAT YOUR DATE? DEPUTY SKINNER?"

Janie leaned against her car and crossed her hands over her chest. "That's none of your business. What's this got to do with your broken-down truck?"

"Just surprised is all. He doesn't seem like your type."

"What is my type?"

"I'm guessing you go for the tattooed, bad boy rather than the true-blue military type. You were a rebel in high school, weren't you?"

"What?" Janie doubled over with laughter. "You don't know me."

"I'm right then?" He moved closer and Janie got the craziest notion that he was about to kiss her.

"What's wrong with your tanker truck?"

"If I knew that, I wouldn't need a mechanic now, would I?"

She laughed. "I'll start working on your equipment first thing tomorrow morning, Chief Griffitt."

He didn't reply right away, just studied her face, and she returned the stare. In the light of the glaring neon sign, he appeared like a Hollywood movie star, his eyes as dark as his beard, tight jeans, and polished boots. She noticed his hands too as he leaned forward and placed an elbow on the car's roof next to her head.

"I'll be by tomorrow then to supervise. I'm not so sure you're qualified for the job."

"I look forward to it," she said, which was absolutely an outright lie. She didn't want the fire chief within one hundred feet of her or anywhere near the county barn. The man was too distracting, and she didn't want any reason to have hope that coming home had been the right thing to do.

Without another word, she spun around, slipped inside her car and drove away. *Do not look back.*

The silhouette of the man standing in the parking lot had not moved, instead, he watched her tail lights.

HER SISTER WAS WAITING up for her, sitting at the bar in the kitchen, in fact.

"Don't you ever go home?" Janie asked as she reached for a cookie jar that always sat at one end of the bar.

Angie lived across the compound in a rundown stucco that had been used to house a ranch hand's family that worked for her grandfather. Angie had made a lot of improvements to make it livable.

"You are greasy and dirty." Angie followed Janie up the stairs to her room, with the cookie jar tucked under one arm.

Janie looked in the mirror and her cheeks grew warm. Did she look that bad when Mack came by the shop? She couldn't deny Angie's accusations. A spot of grease decorated her forehead, and black stains hid under several of her nails. But she was happy. It had been a good day, sinking into the workings of a motor. Grinding on the mower blades until they were sharp enough to slice a tomato.

Angie opened the cookie jar, leaned one hip against the bathroom counter, and pulled out an oatmeal cookie.

"What are you doing here anyway? Just dropped by to criticize?" Janie raised an eyebrow at her younger sis.

"Just dropped in to see what Mom was making for dinner and visit with the folks."

"Don't you cook at your house?"

"Sometimes." Angie helped herself to another cookie.

"I can't believe you're eating that. Taking a break from watching your figure?" Janie observed her sister eat half and then hold out what was left to her. Janie popped it in her mouth without hesitation. "Eating your broken heart away?"

"I'm single. Not broken."

"That's true." Janie laughed. "Me too."

Janie grew uncomfortable with her sister's assessment as Angie looked her up and down. "Are you planning to go out every night?"

"I don't know." Janie shrugged her shoulders and gave her sister an annoyed look. "What's it to you?"

"Where were you?"

"If you must know, Deputy Skinner invited me to eat pizza."

"Jack Skinner from high school? If you're planning to turn into some social butterfly, you need a makeover. I'm calling Chimmi."

"I am not setting foot in a beauty shop. Never met the woman the entire time I lived at home and don't intend to meet her now." Curl Up & Dye in Dixon. She had driven by the shop more than once.

"You have a lot going for you, Janie. There's not an ounce of fat anywhere and your eyes are very pretty. What say we highlight your assets a bit?"

"Enough chit chat. I've got to change into my running shoes." As she took the stairs two at a time, she heard Angie call out.

"I'm making an appointment, and you're going. A good haircut is everything. And besides, it's dusk and almost dark."

Janie's argument was on the tip of her tongue, but then the image of a tall, dark-haired fire chief flashed through her brain. Besides, arguing with Angie was so exhausting. They would keep at it for days until she would finally wear Janie down, and they both knew it.

Angie was the beautiful Olsen sister. Never a hair out of place, coordinated from head to toe, and a smile that lit up every room she walked into. The girl had no enemies and made everyone feel special when she turned that million-watt smile in their direction. Angie was the one who wanted nothing in life but to live out her days on the Rafter O, raising beef steak, and she'd known it since she was a little girl.

As Janie dug in the drawer for her running tights and sports bra, she knew that Angie would win in the end. She took her time giving her sister plenty of time to leave.

"Come running with me," she called out.

The sound of Angie's laughter echoed down the hall and continued down the stairs.

Okay, so she'd get a haircut. Big deal. She could use a trim, and besides, it's not like he would ever ask her out. And if he did, she would never agree to go, not in a million years. So why was her heart thudding like this?

There was no way, no how they would ever be a

couple. So why even think about it? Besides, he was obviously dating Christy from the chamber, which made perfect sense. The little town of Dixon power couple. Both highly involved in the community, and everyone knew them. Of course, they would be in a relationship.

But the yearning to find someone who cared for her never went away. Just like it was in high school, and just like now. Was there any hope against hope that there might be someone out there for her? Someone who might find her attractive despite her flaws? One could dream. But, no, she'd given up on boyfriends years ago. She was tough, opinionated, and too independent. Men liked soft, kind-hearted girls. The kind of women who would make good mothers and homemakers. She could never be like that.

Her mother always told her to talk to God as if He were a friend. Tell Him your troubles, ask for guidance, ask for your deepest heart's desire. Could she dare say it out loud? Watching her parents and their devotion to each other made her heart ache.

She turned the tap off and paused with a hand resting on the sink's edge.

"Please, God. Guide me to the person you have for me." There. She'd said her deepest heart's desire, and knowing that she could be difficult on occasion, she added, "And make me wise enough to recognize him."

Janie swiped the dampness from her eyes caused by the wave of emotion that had swept over her. She pulled a baseball cap tight over her head and twisted her ponytail out the back opening. It was late, but the moon was full, which gave her just enough light to stay in the middle of the road.

11
JANIE

ONE BLOCK FROM THE FOUR-WAY STOP IN Dixon, a long and low stucco building sported a bright yellow awning over the door. Black letters on the front window read Curl Up & Dye.

The cheery yellow outside did nothing to prepare Janie for the inside. The walls were gray, the chairs black, and the carpet was a deep purple. The only lights hung above the mirrors. A sign behind the front counter declared, *WE DO TATTOOS*. The soft scent of vanilla and spice incense surprised her compared with the harsh, bright decor.

After making introductions, Angie hovered close to the beauty shop chair as Janie took a seat. "I'm thinking a medium shade of red, maybe streaked with her natural brown and then some highlights around the face. Can you trim it to curve just below her chin but leave it long in the back?"

"That's just what I was thinking!" Chimmi's eyes sparkled.

Janie watched them both in the mirror. Part of her didn't like allowing these two to call the shots for her, but this scene wasn't really in her wheelhouse. She had to trust that Angie would know what was best for her. Janie looked up at Chimmi, one-half of the Curl Up sisters, as Angie called them. Behind the excessive makeup, the woman was quite attractive. Thin legs, leopard leggings, black leather boots, fuchsia-colored nails. Her violet eyes were rimmed with long eyelashes and black liner. Despite her middle age, her skin was flawless but almost too pale.

Angie mentioned that Chimmi loved experimenting with hair color, which had Janie a little concerned. Every week her hair might be something different, blonde, redhead, spikes, curls. Her sister was the opposite. A little chunky. A little mousey. That's Karmelle. They're both as sweet as can be, which Janie realized to be true. She liked them both immediately. On this day, Chimmi had jet black hair with a white streak over one eye.

"So..." Chimmi slung a cape over her lap, fastened the snaps, and patted Janie's shoulders. "How long are you home for?"

"She's finished her service to our country, and Mom got her a job at the county barn," Angie interjected.

"Doing what?"

"She's a mechanic."

Janie nodded. Angie had been doing the talking for her since she could talk. No reason to break up the system now.

"Oh, good, there's Karmelle. Is there any way you can work me in and do my nails?" Angie smiled sweetly, and, of course, the girl nodded towards her station.

"I'll be right back." Chimmi disappeared into the back

and returned several minutes later with a tray of plastic tubs and foil squares. "What color are we doing? Highlights?"

"I think she needs bright purple or orange highlights," Karmelle added.

Janie must have had an alarmed look on her face because her sister laughed.

"You'll be fine." Angie made her way to the nail table. "I promise. I'll be right over here."

Chimmi smeared goo on separate strands of hair and covered them with a piece of foil. To Janie, the reflection in the mirror resembled something from outer space.

"Okay, you're done. We just need to let it set. Can I get you something to drink?" Chimmi opened a refrigerator close to them.

"No, thank you." Janie didn't see anything but sugary drinks inside.

Chimmi moved a few bottles to the side and held up a squared-off plastic bottle labeled with a picture of a tropical island. "How about sparkling water?"

"That would be nice." Janie smiled.

"I figured you for a health nut." Chimmi gave a deep laugh.

"There's not an ounce of fat on her, that's for sure," Angie called over. "She runs."

Janie's cheeks warmed as they discussed her physique.

"How many miles did you run last night, Janie?" Chimmi cleaned up her station.

"About four."

"Four miles? Why would you do that?" This from Karmelle. She looked up from her work of buffing Angie's forefinger to stare at Janie.

Suddenly the bell over the door tinkled and in walked the fire chief. "Ladies." He scanned the room and his gaze stopped on Janie. He nodded, one corner of his mouth twitching as it seemed he tried to stifle a grin.

Janie's first instinct was to pull the apron over her head to hide her face. Why did it matter that he knew she was at the beauty shop?

"Chief. The hot water heater is in the back." Karmelle showed him the way. "I smelled a hint of gas this morning. I hope it's not leaking."

"I'll take a look at it for you," Mack said.

"Janie ran four miles last night. Can you believe that?" the nail girl piped up.

"Is that right?" A tinge of admiration burned in his eyes.

Janie sat speechlessly. She couldn't think of anything to say, not even a hello. So, she sat in silence, looking like an alien with foil-spiked hair.

Mack nodded at her and walked past towards the back of the salon.

Janie's cheeks burned. When was she going to be finished? How long does color have to stay on anyway? She had never colored her hair in her life, and did not see any reason to start now. She reached behind her and unsnapped the cape, allowing it to slide to the floor.

"What are you doing?"

"I'm going home. I don't have time for this."

"You can't leave until I rinse you out," Chimmi cried out in panic.

"Sit down." Angie demanded. "That's our Janie. She can never sit still for a minute. Be patient. Beauty takes time."

The cape appeared over her shoulders and lap again. "You'll like it. I promise."

Comforting words whispered in her ear, but she didn't believe them. All she could think about was maybe Mack had already left, gone out the back.

When Chimmi moved to one side after resnapping the cape, there he stood looking at her while she stared back. Awkward.

He cleared his throat. "Everything looks good to me, but call if you have any more trouble."

"Thanks, Chief. We sure do appreciate it."

Janie watched him leave, her eyes remaining on him long after the bell tinkled. Through the front picture window, he stopped to chat with a young couple walking by. He opened the door of his truck, but just before getting in, he turned to look back at the beauty shop. Maybe at her? Maybe not. Could he see inside? It felt as though their eyes met.

Janie sighed. She felt ridiculous. As if he would ever notice her. She was dreaming, and the fact that she became tongue-tied when he was in the room made her furious. She frowned and slumped in the chair. Would this day ever be over?

Her mood didn't improve. She barely glanced in the mirror as Chimmi cut, blow-dried, and styled her hair. A wave of hairspray drifted over her head as she closed her eyes and held her breath.

"That is beautiful, Chimmi. Don't you just love it, Janie?" Angie's smile radiated.

Janie nodded without even looking at herself in the mirror. No amount of hair color or highlights would ever change her face from plain to pretty. What was the use? She followed Angie to the Rafter O truck.

"Now what?" she asked. "Oh, and thanks for treating me to the new hairdo."

"I'm going to a roping. Why don't you come with me?"

"No, just take me home."

12

CHIMMI

As she swept hair clippings on the floor into a little pile, Chimmi said, "That girl's got it bad."

"Uh, huh. She just don't know it yet. Did you see how she looked at him? And he looked back! There was electricity. They seriously need to be together. But doesn't he already have a girlfriend?" Her sister Karmelle grinned in a mischievous way.

"Well, we can fix that. Not a problem." Chimmi took on a serious look.

"You're darn tootin' we can." Excitement showed on Karmelle's face.

"First things first, we gotta come up with something to keep Christy busy at the chamber. Too busy to have time for the fire chief." Chimmi swept the pile of hair into her dustpan and tossed the collection into the trash can.

In unison, the sisters said, "Out of sight, out of mind."

Chimmi plopped down in one of her customer's

chairs and twirled it to face Nancy, who sat under a dryer, and Waldeen, who relaxed in a guest chair.

The door buzzed, and in walked Belinda from the coffee shop.

She stopped and stared at them. "What's going on? I know that look. You're up to no good. You girls are planning something. And whoever is the target of your meddling will not survive."

They all giggled.

"Spill. Who is it?" Belinda asked.

"Do you know Janie Olsen?" Karmelle was right in there, excited.

Belinda put her purse in Chimmi's chair. "Olsen? She kin to Nathan and Angie?"

"Yes, their sister. I didn't know till today they had a sister named Janie. I remembered Libbie is away at college." Chimmi took on the leadership role in their little ring of mischief.

"Yes, Janie. She's next to the oldest, Nathan. Then there's Angie. And Libbie. Travis is the youngest," another customer piped up. "He married Destynee Raleigh."

"Didn't realize they had another sister until I met her today." Chimmi squinted her eyes and reached for the glasses around her neck on a beaded chain.

"Yes, Plain Jane. That's what they called her in school." Belinda eased into a zebra-striped chair. I just don't remember what the girl looks like. Is she really that plain?" Belinda tilted her head to the side.

"She was in the military and is back home now. She's really fit. Nice figure. And Chimmi just did a makeover. She's not plain anymore. Those highlights really brightened up her face." Karmelle smiled, proud of her sister.

"We need an event. An event so big that Christy at

the chamber is too busy to mind her boyfriend." Chimmi said.

Belinda stood to pace around the small shop. Silence reigned. She paused at a yellowed newspaper article hanging on the wall in a glass frame.

"I didn't know your grandmother opened this shop? Is this building really that old?"

"Even older than that, actually," Karmelle said.

"It was one of the original houses built when the town was founded. It used to be the post office and then a feed store, until our grandmother opened her shop," Chimmi said.

"How old is this town?"

"Our great-great-grandpa and the Olsens were some of the first settlers."

"What year was that?"

"I'll have to do the math, but I'm guessing the early 1900s or so?"

For several minutes each beauty customer disappeared into her own thoughts.

Eyes opened wide, some sat straight up in their chairs, and in unison, they said, "Founders' Day."

"We'll have a Founders' Day celebration to beat all Founders' Days." Belinda's eyes sparkled.

"But what year is it?" Karmelle asked.

"Who cares? We can fudge that." Chimmi saw no reason to delay true love based on insignificant details.

"Yeah, but you usually celebrate a milestone year, like fifty or seventy-five or a hundred," Karmelle argued.

"I'll head to the chamber and ask Christy to look it up. Plant the seed that we need a celebration. It's the perfect excuse to keep her occupied." Belinda grabbed her bag and quickly said to Chimmi, "Put me down for an appointment tomorrow. I need a trim." Before they knew it, she was gone with the door banging shut behind her.

"Now, all we have to do is get Janie Olsen and her fire chief within one hundred feet of each other." Chimmi enjoyed a challenge and always had great expectations of what she hoped to accomplish.

"That's going to be harder than it sounds," Karmelle said.

"Always raining on my parade, dear sister. We can do this. Just you wait and see."

Chimmi opened a diet soda and settled in one of her chairs with a twinkle in her eyes.

"Remember when my Freddy came along, Karmelle? He was handsome and had dark hair like Chief Mack. We were young when he had dark hair, that is." She gave a chuckle, then got serious. "You didn't think he was right for me back then."

"It wasn't that." Karmelle sat next to her, voice low. The other ladies in the shop tried to listen however, discreetly.

"What was it then? Were you jealous because you didn't have a boyfriend at the time and I did?"

"No, Chimmi. Well, maybe a little." She shrugged her shoulders and grinned. "I just didn't know him yet. And... and..." A tear formed in Karmelle's eye, and with a finger she pushed it away. "I was afraid everything would change if you dated him. That he'd take you away from me. And he did."

"Oh, Karmelle. He had to go where the jobs were. We were only away for a while. Then we came back when our folks got sick."

"But everything did change, Chimmi. Grandma died. Ma and Pa died. I was all alone."

"I'm sorry, Karmelle. That's why you searched for love, and ended up in San Antonio."

"You can say it. I had a lot of boyfriends. Most of them flakes."

"That's why I want to help Janie and Mack. They're two good people, and both have been hurt. The whole town knows Mack's story about losing his dad. I'm not sure about Janie's, but you can just see the pain on her face. Maybe she's never had a real beau. But everyone needs love, Karmelle. And we can help her. Just like Grandma and Ma helped me. Now I know they were nudging, and maybe even scheming behind the scenes. Maybe that's where I get it from."

Chimmi smiled and reached over for her sister's hand. "And don't worry, it's not too late for us either. I've got my eye on two men in town who just might be our knights in shining armor."

Karmelle let out a squawking laugh. "Oh, my goodness! Now you've got to be kidding. You had better not be doing any such thing. I'm just fine as a spinster. And there's no such thing as princes... only frogs if you ask me."

The customers were all openly smiling. "What are y'all talkin' about?" one of them asked.

"Oh, Chimmi is just being her normal self—matchmaking for everyone in town." Karmelle held her sister's hand tight. "I love you," she said quietly.

"Back atcha, Sis."

63

13
JANIE

JANIE RODE NEXT TO HER SISTER IN SILENCE and she could tell Angie's feelings were hurt. She wasn't the sort who gushed over a hairstyle. Maybe she could at least have pretended to be excited for her sister's sake. But she had never been good at fake feelings. Without a word between them, Angie pulled to a stop in front of Rafter O Ranch headquarters.

"Thanks," Janie said. "I'm going to hit the pavement."

After changing, Janie hurried back downstairs and stopped at the sink to fill her water bottle. Glancing out the window, she saw her mom pulling weeds in her fall garden. Her father walked up behind her and offered his hand to help her up. They hugged, standing in each other's arms for longer than necessary, but clinging to one another anyway. Her mom's eyes were closed as a peaceful smile formed on her lips.

Their love and dedication to each other was the reason the Rafter O Ranch was so successful. No matter what they faced, good or bad, they always maintained a solid front.

Without another glance towards her parents, she walked out the back door, avoiding the yard so as not to disturb their moment, and jogged toward the open road.

She almost gave into Angie and went to the roping, but, for years, she had sat on the bleachers watching her brothers and sister ride back and forth, swirling the rope overhead. When she got big enough, her parents let her drive the four-wheeler that pulled the metal roping dummy shaped like a calf. At least she felt a part of the family then, but that was as far as it went.

AFTER JANIE'S RUN, she passed through the kitchen, to the family den, and into toddler chaos. Both of her nephews were there. Her youngest brother's son, Wyatt, and her oldest brother's son, Gabriel. Almost a year apart, they had become enthralled with each other even though Wyatt was only a few months old. Janie could imagine them becoming best friends when they got old enough to run around.

Better than watching the boys play was seeing the delight on her parents' faces as they gazed at their grandsons. It was a huge blessing that her father was alive after his recent health scare. And now, here he was, enjoying the boys. It could have turned out much worse.

She planted a kiss on each of the boys' heads and ran upstairs.

After stepping out of the shower, she flipped her head upside down and dried her hair, not really focusing on the color. She spun around to look in the mirror and had to do a double-take. The vibrant colors of brown, red, and blonde were shiny, and framed her face perfectly. It wasn't bad. And it did make her eyes show up more.

She bounded back downstairs to oohs and ahs at whatever cartoon Gabriel was selecting on the television.

"Gabe," her brother Nathan said, "take it easy with that remote. Grandpa won't like it if you break it."

It was good to be back home with her family. But still, that nagging feeling of being different from them bothered her. The military had taught her to face a challenge head-on, so she was determined to "make nice" with her brothers, their kids, and the rest of the family. She would try to fit in, but conversation wasn't easy. They had nothing in common. She had resigned herself to the fact that she would probably never marry or have kids, and horses had never appealed to her. It was as if she had been born to the wrong family.

Janie sat on the floor near Gabriel, who had set the remote down and was now pressing his eye against his baby cousin's eye, making Wyatt squeal with delight. She laughed.

"They are very entertaining, aren't they?" Nathan laughed too.

Their mother came in from the kitchen and addressed her youngest, who sat in a chair checking his phone. "Travis, it's time for Wyatt's bottle and then to bed for him. Maybe Janie would like to feed him."

Travis hardly acknowledged, only gave a grunt of sorts.

Janie's eyes displayed a slight panic. "I don't know, Mom. I don't really know much about babies. Where's Destynee?"

Mr. Olsen spoke up from his chair with a grin and raised eyebrows. "Maybe it's time you learned about them. You might be having one someday."

"What?" Janie scrunched her face at her father.

"Leave the girl alone, Skip." The mother picked up the baby and reached towards Janie. "Here, I'll tell you what to do. Support his head. Take the bottle and just nudge the tip between his lips. He'll do the rest. It's easy." Then to Gabriel, she chastised him for poking at the baby. "Now, Gabriel, leave him alone while he has his bottle. Then it's night-night for the both of you."

No one ever answered about the whereabouts of Wyatt's mother, Destynee. She was a wannabe country singer. Maybe she was off singing or something. Janie had heard there was a weird story there, with a pushy stage mom and everything.

When she was in the military, Janie endured tough training and even some dangerous situations. But holding this tiny human was more intimidating than anything she had ever done before. She didn't want to hurt him or break him and only wanted to do an excellent job.

Her mother smiled at her. "See. You're doing great."

"If you say so. He's so little."

The baby felt warm to her. Not feverishly warm, just a warm, living being. It was kind of incredible to think about. She was an aunt now, and she wanted to be a good one. She imagined the boys older, growing up, playing sports in school, riding horses. Janie wanted to be there for them, and she wanted them to like her. Maybe she'd teach them about running. She'd leave the horses to Angie.

As if telepathically sending her signals, Angie entered the room.

"Well, look at you, playing Mom." She didn't smile and Janie felt there might still be a little tension between them.

"Hey, Angie," she forced herself to be friendly. "Yeah, look at what Mom has gotten me into."

"Well, at least your hair looks good while you're doing it." Angie's cocky sense of humor came forth.

A little embarrassed when her father and brothers turned to look at her with questioning expressions, she lowered her eyes to the baby. But she was determined to smile and even give a little laugh. "Yeah, I guess so. Thanks to you, Angie."

Janie was glad when her sister gave a slight nod in her direction, and more so when their mother came to take the baby from her.

"Time for Wyatt to go beddy-bye. He finished the bottle. You did good, Janie. Oh, Angie, if you want anything from the kitchen, help yourself. We all had some dessert earlier."

"Thanks, Mom, I just might. I don't have anything at my place."

Janie kissed Wyatt's forehead and handed him back to her mother, then followed Angie into the kitchen, hoping to give her a real apology for not making a fuss over the hair earlier.

Angie had sliced a piece of pie for herself and was pouring a glass of milk. She looked at Janie and asked, "Want any?"

"No. Thanks anyway."

"Oh, right, you just came from a run."

"Angie, I wanted to apologize about the hair."

"What? You don't like it?"

"No, I do. And I appreciate your going with me. I just felt that maybe you were upset because I didn't get as excited as you did about it."

"Well, you were kinda short on enthusiasm. And you yanked off your cape and tried to make a run for it. Then you didn't even want to go to the roping with me. Can you blame me for being a little perturbed with you? I'm just trying to help you, Janie."

"Angie, try to see it from my point of view. I've never had my hair colored before. And I'm not used to those ladies in the shop making a fuss. On top of everything... that, uh... *man* saw me with foils in my hair, probably looking like an alien or something. I'm sure he had a good laugh later."

"What man? Oh, Chief Mack? Well, who cares what he thinks? And you'll have to get used to the foil thing in your hair. We all look like aliens during that process. It's the price we pay for beauty." Angie let out one of her big laughs and Janie couldn't help but give a small smirk. After a few seconds of silence, it was as though a light-bulb went off in Angie's head. "Oh... *you* care what he thinks. Is that it?"

"What who thinks?"

"Chief Mack. You know who we're talking about. You think he's hot." Now Angie was grinning from ear to ear.

"I do not. In fact, he's infuriating. Every time I've run into him, he makes me mad."

"Uh, huh... *madly* in love."

"Angie, stop it."

"Janie's got a crush..." she said in a sing-songy voice.

"Be quiet. What are you? Thirteen? I don't want the guys to hear you."

"Well, then it's our little secret. And you know what that means, don't you?

"What?"

"You owe me. Big time." Angie wiggled her brows and grinned to emphasize she had the upper hand now.

14
JANIE

MONDAY WENT BY WITHOUT A HITCH, JUST THE way Janie liked it. She'd changed the oil in the sheriff's SUV, tuned up a county dump truck, and reorganized the supply shed, making a detailed list of materials on hand. As she washed her hands, a glance at the clock, which read a few minutes before five, surprised her. She stared at the clock again to make sure. The day had flown by and she had forgotten to stop for lunch.

Mack never showed up with his tanker truck, so her jittery nerves were for nothing.

Right as she was thinking that, the low, deep-throated vibration of a Harley made her frown. She wasn't supposed to work on employees' vehicles in the county-owned barn. The human resources gal had been adamant about that. Apparently, there had been issues in the past with previous employees. She flung the hand towel into the trash and turned to whoever it might be, prepared to explain that the shop was closed. She was ready to call it a day.

The sight in the parking lot made her stop in her tracks.

Swinging one long leg over the seat was Mack wearing black leathers, stretching his arms overhead to remove his helmet. She couldn't see his eyes behind reflecting sunglasses, but her heart thudded anyway.

"Let's go for a ride," he said as he lifted a helmet out of the storage trunk on the back of the bike and held it out to her.

She pretended confidence and sass, but couldn't think of a catchy reply. Tongue-tied instead, she felt like melting into a puddle on the cement floor. And even worse, she froze in place, staring without answering.

He walked closer and closer, and stopped just in front of her with a questioning look in his eyes. "Well?"

"I d-d-din't bring a change of clothes," she stammered.

"I assume you're wearing something under those overalls." An eyebrow raised in a mischievous look.

No strength to argue, and truth be told, she did not want to, she only nodded her head and spun on one heel to slip into the office. Unzipping the county-issued overalls, she stepped out of them and hung them on a hook behind the door. She had worn jeans that day and a camouflage-patterned tank top, but had forgotten to grab a jacket on her way out this morning. Steel-toed black work boots would have to do, and she tossed her ball cap on the desk but left her hair in a ponytail.

Appearing back into the garage, Mack was frozen in place this time, assessing her over from head to toe with his eyes.

"I think you'll need this." He shrugged off his leather jacket and nodded his head towards the bike. "Ready?"

71

Except she was tongue-tied again at the sight of his black T-shirt that stretched over a broad chest, leading down to tanned and lean bare forearms. She blinked to break the spell and took the jacket from his outstretched hand. It hung heavy and warm on her shoulders and smelled all male. He slipped the helmet over her head and buckled the chin strap. A little embarrassed at his closeness, she backed away and then turned to stop again at the sight of his bike. Chrome laced wheels, pull-back handlebars, silver fenders, with a black seat and black trunk.

"A Harley-Davidson Road King Firefighter Special Edition in red!" She did not hide her admiration. "Nice ride."

Surprise flashed in his eyes for a split second, and then his face held a certain amount of pride. He didn't respond to her comment. Without saying another word, she waited until he was seated before swinging a leg over the bike and settling in behind him. She leaned back, keeping a distance between her body and his. The comfortable seat surprised her. If she didn't know any better, she'd think she was at home in her dad's recliner.

"I'm not contagious," he said with a chuckle. "You can put your arms around me."

She complied and wished she hadn't. She leaned against his back, solid and strong, and could feel his taut stomach with her fingertips. Her whole being was a quiver.

The Harley roared to life, the sound reverberating between the buildings as Mack turned onto Main Street. He revved the engine at the four-way stop. The Dixon city limits sign flashed in her line of vision for a split second as they shot forward onto the open county road. She had forgotten to ask where they were going.

The land passed by in shades of brown and gold. The

sight of the parched ground made her think about the pasture fire and how desperate ranchers were for rain. If this were a movie, the moment would make for a perfect ending. Riding on a Harley of all things with a handsome fire chief. What girl wouldn't want that?

Janie had been obsessed with Harley-Davidson bikes her entire life, although she had never owned one. She had ridden on the back of one before with a friend's father, an experience that inspired her to learn everything she could about the company and their products. Janie closed her eyes. The power vibrated in her legs. There was no way to know how fast they were going, but the ride was smooth and the engine worked effortlessly.

The thrill of riding a piece of American history made her want to shout. The adrenaline rush was something she would not soon forget. Maybe she should use her savings to buy a Harley and then take a cross-country trip. She could join HOG, Harley Owners Group, and spend the next few months on the open road. The man she held onto could be part of that dream as well. To have someone to share the sights and adventure of a road trip, traveling Route 66 would be the ultimate dream come true.

The spell broke like a popped balloon in her brain and heart when she reminded herself who she was. Plain Janes don't get to ride off into the sunset on the back of a motorcycle with the man of their dreams. And that realization made her wonder why he had stopped by to pick her up in the first place. Whatever this was would be fleeting. There was no future here, no possibility of her ever sharing a life with any man, particularly one like Mack Griffitt.

She had discovered a long time ago that living in the moment brought peace to her spirit. There was no sense in worrying over what would never be, so she tried to enjoy the blessings of life as they came. She closed her eyes, focusing on the power and thrill of riding on a piece of Americana as it glided along and the solid nearness of a man who had offered to give her a ride on his Harley.

That was enough for now.

15

JANIE

JANIE SNUGGLED AGAINST MACK'S BACK, turning her head to rest her helmet against him as he merged onto the interstate highway. She tried to relax and not make this anything more than it was. Just two friends, taking a ride on a Harley. And then he exited off the highway and turned south. His helmet prevented her from asking where they were going. She tried to focus on the feel of the smooth bike and the scenery. They had been driving for about an hour, which was fine by her, and she liked that they were traveling slowly. Some Harleys were made for taking the open road at a much easier speed instead of racing to be somewhere. Cruising, they called it. She wouldn't mind if they stayed like this all night. Away from the dusty-covered town she had come back to. Away from the knowing glances from her mother and the prying eyes of her sister. Just away.

He turned onto the road that dead-ended at the Palo Duro Canyon State Park, a deep chasm in the flat Texas Panhandle, carved out by the Prairie Dog Town Fork of the Red River. He paid the park attendant and they eased into the state park between thick mesquite until parts of the canyon came into view. Instead of stopping at the observation point and Visitor's Center located on the top edge of the canyon, he followed the switchback road that wound towards the bottom. At one end of the curve, he pulled off on the blacktop pavement and parked, the rumbling replaced by a peaceful melody of birds.

Janie removed her helmet and closed her eyes, allowing the healing powers of nature to settle over her like a warm quilt. She took a breath and smiled when she recognized the trill of a bobwhite quail. When she opened her eyes, Mack stood nearby, watching her intently with an amused look. She met his stare, while trying to ignore the tingling in the pit of her stomach.

"Are you going to sit there all night?"

She laughed and hopped off the back, shrugging the jacket from her back. Mack took her helmet and stowed everything in the trunk, turning the lock with a key. She stood still to make a mental note of the tingling in her behind. Another unique trait known among Harley-Davidson riders.

"This way." he said.

She followed him along a red dirt trail that led into a thicket of mesquite and brush. Her boots grew heavy as she trudged behind him, and before too long, her brow was damp with sweat. They emerged from behind an ancient mesquite to stand on a cliff's edge. A small lookout. The length of the colorful canyon stretched out before them. Colors of orange, purple, and light gray layered the sides of the deep chasm that rose upwards to seventy feet from the riverbed plain. Mesquite trees, cedars, and juniper jumbled the bottom. The sight took her breath away. She must have gasped because he turned to look at her.

"You've never been here before?"

"Once, when I was very little. We brought some visiting relatives for a cookout and hike. Why had I forgotten about this place?"

"I ride my Harley out here every chance I get. It's quiet, relaxing."

"Your girlfriend must enjoy the scenery. What's her name? Christy? Do you guys come here a lot?"

He looked away, then quietly answered. "She doesn't like the bike. I've invited her several times and she always says no, so I don't ask anymore."

She turned to look at him but didn't say a word. It was obvious she had touched upon a personal subject.

He followed a path towards a large boulder and they sat next to each other.

"You take on a lot of responsibility in our little town of Dixon, don't you?"

He paused before answering, gazing out over the canyon. "I'm trying to carry on my father's work. He was so involved in the community. I can never hold a candle to him, but I'm trying."

"What happened?" By the look on Mack's face, Janie realized there might be more to the story than she knew.

"He died in a fire trying to save some kids. He had to help the mom out first, who was big and pregnant. And then he went back in for the kids. His partner told me they were so scared and huddled in one corner and that they wouldn't come when they helped their mom. Dad's partner took the mom, and my father went back to the bedroom for the kids, but the roof collapsed on them before they could get everybody out."

"Were you there?"

"I should have been. I usually went on every call with him, but not that time."

"I'm very sorry for your loss." She laid a hand on his shoulder. Her heart went out to this handsome fire chief who still carried the burden of his father's memory. He seemed intense and weary for a man so young.

They remained side by side, a comfortable silence between them. Not feeling the need for conversation, Janie felt at ease close to him. They watched the fading colors of the sunset as the light disappeared from the sky.

"What about you?" Mack broke the silence. "What's your sad tale?"

"Nothing sad really. I got out of this town as soon as I could, did a tour in the military, and now I'm back. No future plans. Just hanging out until I can figure out what I want to do with the rest of my life."

"No boyfriend?"

That question surprised her. "No."

"Are you hungry?"

She stifled a giggle. That was a sudden jump of topics.

"One more minute." She did not want to leave, and she hated that small talk had broken the spell of the moment. She didn't want to say something stupid, and in the fading light her face was hidden. It would be dark soon. That eased her self-consciousness.

He sighed. She could feel the tension roll off him like a tidal wave.

"Are you dating the deputy?"

"What?" Her eyes wide with surprise, she peered at him in the semi-darkness.

"At the pizza joint. Are you going out again with the deputy?"

She paused to think about how to answer that question, and mainly wondered why he would be asking.

"I don't know. Maybe."

"How did the trip to the beauty shop turn out?" he added with a chuckle. "You looked miserable sitting in that chair."

Couldn't the man keep quiet for just a few more seconds? But she had to ask, "Why were you at the beauty shop anyway?"

"They called me about a possible gas leak on the hot water heater."

"Fire chiefs don't get the weekend off?"

"Rarely. In the town of Dixon, fire chiefs are never off duty. Comes with the territory."

She laughed in the pitch darkness. "How are we going to hike out?"

"We can use our phones. I'm hungry. How about you?"

She certainly wouldn't argue against a meal. They walked slowly back to the bike and put on their helmets. It was too dark to continue further into the canyon, so Mack turned back towards the entrance to the park. They hit the open road again and he sped towards Amarillo. Within no time, he had parked beside a row of bikes in front of Smokey Bill's Grill on historic Route 66.

"You hang out at a biker bar?"

"They have the best burgers for miles around. You'll see."

She smiled at his reply, and then her stomach reminded her she had not taken a lunch break. She placed her helmet on the handlebar and stretched her arms overhead.

"Wait a minute," he said. "There's one thing you should do."

"What's that?"

"I'm just curious about that haircut you seemed so

frustrated over. I'd like to see how it turned out." He reached up and gently pulled the scrunchy off her pony-tail, running his fingers through her hair as it tumbled to her shoulders.

His eyes drifted over her hair and then stopped at her face. For a split second, panic hit the pit of her stomach. He leaned closer, staring at her lips. Was he going to kiss her?

"I like it," he said as he turned to hold open an old-fashioned screen door.

She ran her fingers through her hair to shake out the kinks and, on jiggly legs, walked into a covered patio area. Every table was full, so she continued on inside, where she was greeted by the smells of charbroiled beef. Neon signs advertising everything from beer to aspirin covered every available space of the rough-hewn paneled walls, some hanging from the ceiling. The noise of live musicians huddled in a far corner playing their hearts out and a chatty crowd was a relief for her riled-up emotions. She preferred a table right in the noisy middle of the ruckus, but no such luck. The smiling hostess led them to a back corner table.

16

MACK

SOUNDS FROM THE LIVE BAND MADE IT difficult for much conversation, which did not matter anyway, because Mack could hardly keep his eyes off Janie. The waitress took their order.

"Sweet tea," he said.

"No beer?" Janie asked in surprise.

"I could get a call at any minute. I don't drink during the spring and summer, high fire season. If the ground is good and wet with snow, I might consider it, but otherwise my job doesn't end at five o'clock."

They settled into a back corner table at Smokey Bill's Grill. Janie leaned her back against the wall and stretched her legs out on the other chair, turning her full attention to the band that played at the far end of the dining hall.

When she had appeared from the shop office without those bulky overalls, in that tank top and skin-tight jeans, Mack had almost passed out. There wasn't an ounce of fat on her wiry, muscled body. Janie was so the opposite of his girlfriend, Christy, who was tall enough to look him in the eye, but delicate and needy.

81

Christy was kind and giggly and curvy, all the things he imagined he liked in a woman. He had almost proposed on Valentine's Day, but something held him back. He loved Christy, didn't he? They had known each other since they were kids, grown up together, she was the cheerleader, and he was the quarterback. The whole town assumed they would marry, but they had not started dating until later in life. But every time he was with her, he felt empty, like there was something more waiting around the bend. Something just out of his reach. Something he could not define.

And now, other things invaded his thoughts, like a bundle of energy hopping out of the county's road grader. The fact that she knew what type of Harley he drove and did not hide her admiration for his ride had shocked him. Without hesitation, she climbed on the back of the bike. Having her behind him on his Harley felt like the missing piece he had been searching for his whole life.

Janie held back from him. He could tell. She did not trust easily, and he wasn't sure who had broken her heart, but she was wounded. He had wracked his brain, and for the life of him, he could not remember her from high school. In fact, he kept forgetting to ask her last name. But it didn't matter. For now, it was enough that she was here, across the table from him, watching the band.

Mack laughed when she took the first bite of her burger. A complete look of satisfaction came over her face as she chewed.

"It's good, huh?"

She smiled and nodded, accompanied by appreciative sounds of "Mmmm, uhmmm..." She even closed her eyes as though in hamburger heaven. A dab of mustard remained on her upper lip. He wanted to wipe it off for her but refrained. He just pointed to his own lip, and she got the message and swiped her mouth with a napkin.

The music stopped as the band filed off the stage for a break, replaced by the chatter and clinking of people eating.

"Tell me about your dad," she said.

"He was larger than life with a heart of gold. His dream was to be a fireman, from his earliest years. Fighting fires was what he always wanted to do."

"That's admirable."

"With that responsibility came even more involvement in the community. People got used to seeing him everywhere, and when they needed something, they would call my dad because they knew he would help them. If your driveway was snow-packed, Dad knew someone with a backhoe. Electric lines down. Dad knew the service supervisor."

"I'm sorry to say, I don't remember him. High school seems like a blur to me now."

"Where did you live?"

"Out in the country," was all she offered. "My brothers and sisters were more into ranch work, and I liked to run. Or my nose was buried in a book."

"I just don't remember you from high school. I guess we were there at the same time?"

"I was on the cross-country track team, so like I said, most of my spare time was spent running by myself along the county roads. Not much in my childhood to tell." She leaned forward to sip tea through the straw, avoiding his glance.

He watched her. "The band's pretty good, isn't it?"

"Yeah. They are." She wiped her mouth, paused to look into his eyes, and then asked, "What about your mom? Is she around?"

"Right now, she's visiting her sister in Amarillo. They get along like kids and are always doing some fun thing or helping others. I'm glad, because when my dad died, my mom was a basket case for a long time."

"What about siblings?"

"I'm the oldest. I have a brother in ranching, and my little sister is away at college."

"Wow," she said, "mine too. Youngest brother is a horse trainer, and one sister is at college."

They both smiled at their shared family status. He didn't think to ask about her other siblings. He was too busy looking at her.

"I'm glad your mother is doing well. That must've been a tough time. For everyone."

Mack nodded slightly as he looked at her pretty hair, her sparkling eyes. He didn't understand it, but he felt comfortable with her, like he could talk to her about anything. He knew she'd listen. Sometimes Christy seemed self-absorbed. And she was into fashion, always wanting to look her best and stay clean. Janie was pretty much the opposite and seemed to care less about that stuff. He liked that.

"We should do this again sometime," he said, secretly hoping he could stop by every day after she got off work.

"That sounds nice. I'd like that."

"Great, but not this weekend. I have a few county obligations "

"Is there anything in the county that you leave for someone else to do?"

He laughed. "Now that you mention it, not really."

She grinned and rolled her eyes in a tease.

They both pushed back from the table and held their stomachs. He picked up her ticket along with his and left cash on the table.

"That was really good. Thanks for the treat. You didn't have to do that. I could have paid my way."

"My pleasure. One, my dad always taught me to treat a lady. And two, I learned long ago that it's best to keep the mechanic happy. You get better service that way." He chuckled.

"Oh really? I think they call that bribery." There was a trace of laughter in her voice. "I'll have you know, I do not accept bribes. I do accept hamburgers though."

"I figured you for a protein gal. No doughnuts, right?" He surveyed her arms.

"I try to steer clear of sugar."

"So that means no nightcap? Ice cream, I mean."

"No, thanks though. And actually, I think it's time I got home."

"I guess the lady is telling me she's about to turn into a pumpkin. Okay, your chariot awaits."

Outside they hopped on his bike. He liked the way she right away clung to his middle and leaned into the turns with him.

When they reached town, he stopped the motorcycle beside her car, where she had left it parked by the mechanic's shop. He shut the bike off and let her climb off first. Then he put the kickstand down, got off, and stood in front of her.

She suddenly seemed a little unsure, nervous even. He was thinking about kissing her, couldn't think of anything else, but instead said, "Hope you had a good time. Thanks for going with me."

She nodded but looked down at the asphalt. "Thanks for the ride. And dinner."

And then she put her hand out to him. Was she going to shake hands? This was a little odd. Like they were ending a business meeting.

He wasn't sure what to do, and he didn't want to embarrass her. So, he took her hand and shook it.

"I'll let you know about that truck. Goodnight."

"Goodnight, Janie." It was the only thing that came into his foggy brain to say. He should have kissed her. He wanted to kiss her.

He should have kept driving. Nothing had ever felt more right than riding his Harley with Janie behind him.

17

CHIMMI

THE CURL UP SISTERS LEANED SIDE BY SIDE against the counter in their shop. At a certain time of the day, the sun hit the big picture window out front and reflected the letters of the business onto the back wall, creating a hazy *Curl Up & Dye*. That had been Chimmi's late husband's idea. She smiled every time she looked at it, and thought of him at that exact moment every single day. There was a time when the image had brought tears instead of a smile.

The smell of hairspray still hung in the air. The work day was nearly done. Chimmi would go to her lonely house, and Karmelle would go to her lonely house, not on the same street but right behind each other across the alley. Although it might seem weird for them to eat dinner together after spending the whole day at the beauty shop working, oftentimes, they did. They had fun trying new recipes and packing leftovers for lunch. With all of their family gone, it felt comforting to Chimmi to have her sister close again in their soon-to-be twilight years.

"There has got to be some kind of event going on in this county where we can get both of them there." Chimmi said, after she'd smiled at the wall. Her wall. "The fire chief and the mechanic are meant for each other."

"Nothing goes on. I keep trying to tell you that. Why you convinced me to move here is beyond me. We could be in San Antonio right now on the riverwalk. I had that primo property all locked in." Karmelle delicately filed a neon pink nail to a sharp point.

"How you even manage with those claws is beyond me. That property would have broken you, and you know it. The only thing that saved your butt from bankruptcy was me offering you a booth space here."

"I had a good client base that was growing. It might have taken me a few years, but I could have made it work." The younger sister started to display a pouty face.

"You were miserable, Karmelle. Your heart was broken, and it was never going to mend in San Antonio."

No argument there, the silence interrupted by the scritch, scritch of a nail file. Her comment was met with silence.

Chimmi continued, "I want everyone to be happy. Life is too short to spend even one minute in misery. In Dixon, you have no pressure. No debt hanging over your head. Besides, I'm glad you're here."

She gave her sister an admiring glance. "I'm glad to be here too," Karmelle said, "but I'll never understand your incessant need to get involved in everybody's business. It's not like you have an obligation to make sure everyone finds their destiny. You don't owe the world anything, Chimmi."

"I know it, but it's what I do. God has a plan for everyone, and sometimes people need a little nudge. I'm just trying to be His hands and feet doing His work. One of His vessels. Isn't that what we're supposed to do? Now, about the two wayward souls that can't find their way to each other. There has *got* to be something coming up where we can get those two together. There's always something going on in this town."

"If you say so. You've made good work of keeping Christy busy at the chamber with the Founders' Day celebration."

"The fire chief is a tough one. He's too busy as it is, and he would know if I suddenly invented a reason for him to be somewhere."

Karmelle nodded her head in agreement. "And that Olsen girl is a smart one. She'll see right through your manipulation."

The door buzzed as Christy walked in.

"Speak of the devil," Karmelle mumbled under her breath.

"Good evening," Chimmi smiled brightly. "What can we help you with today?"

"I know this is last minute, but can you give me a quick trim? And I need a manicure in the worst way. I have a meeting with a historian who might give me some leads on the county. I'm trying to compile as much county history as I can to write press releases about our Founders' Day celebration."

"That's a great idea, Christy. Spread the news across the Texas Panhandle."

"That's what I'm hoping for."

"We would be happy to work you in. We have about thirty minutes until our next scheduled appointment. Have a seat." She waved an arm towards the back. "Let's get you shampooed."

"What color polish?" Karmelle called out after her.

"Something professional. Smart. Something that suits a chamber president."

"*Sky Blue*? *Purple Promise*? Oh, how about *Fiery Red Dragon*?" Karmelle giggled.

"Pale pink with white tips," Chimmi answered, giving Karmelle a somewhat stern face.

"Boring and dull." Karmelle made a face and, with a heavy sigh, dug through her drawer. She kept the boring colors at the very back.

Christy appeared from the washroom with a towel wrapped around her head. "The only problem is, I'll have to miss the livestock show this weekend."

"Stock show?" Karmelle asked with raised eyebrows.

Chimmi knew she could care less, but as with most beauty workers, they were experts at keeping the clients talking. People loved talking about themselves. Chimmi and Karmelle knew everyone's secrets.

"It's a huge weekend at the county rodeo grounds," Christy bubbled. "We had over two hundred entries last year. Sheep, goats, chickens, and of course, cows. All those 4-H kids work so hard during the year."

"Maybe I should check it out," Karmelle said as she worked her magic on Christy's nails. "Why are you so hard on your nails? You need cuticle oil, too."

"I have some in my desk."

"It doesn't work, if you don't use it." Karmelle tilted her head and gave her a side glance.

Chimmi combed out the girl's blonde hair. "These ends are bad. You could use some conditioner too."

"Just a trim, and I don't have time for any conditioner. Blow me dry, and I'll be on my way. I have to run to Amarillo and pick up the trophies."

"So, you're running into the city today, and then back

again on Saturday? Our little community keeps you busy, doesn't it?" Chimmi brushed the girl's hair.

Christy laughed as she glanced in the mirror at Chimmi. "Yes, but I love my job. One of you wouldn't mind helping Mack hand out prizes, would you? It's Saturday afternoon just before they serve the bar-b-que."

"I bet one of us could do that." Chimmi met her sister's eyes and winked. "Couldn't we, Karmy?"

"Don't see why not, Chi Chi." With a giggle she held up a bottle of neon turquoise polish. Christy and Chimmi shook their heads no. "Saving this one for me then, for Saturday. Think I'll drag my turquoise jewelry out too."

"I agree with Chimmi. Just simple and neat nails look more professional. I want to make a good impression. Even though this historian is probably eighty or better, I want him to take me seriously. This part of the state has so much history, and our town of Dixon is no exception. You would be surprised." Christy continued to chat about the families and ranches who first settled in the area and all she had learned since beginning her research.

"Sounds like you've done your homework." Chimmi deftly wielded her scissors through Christy's locks. "It's going to be a Founders' Day celebration they'll talk about for years to come."

"That's my goal." Christy gently blew on freshly polished nails, while Karmelle worked on the other hand.

Chimmi used the roller brush and blow-dryer to shape her hair. "How about a little spray?"

"Sure. Thank you." Christy shut her eyes as Chimmi sent a few quick spritzes of hairspray into the atmosphere around them. She stood back to admire her work. Christy was a beautiful girl, inside and out, but she wasn't the girl for Mack. Chimmi knew it down in her soul. Mack had suffered a lot in his young life, had to grow up early after the fire that killed his dad, and he had settled into the footprints, taking over as fire chief after leaving college before he graduated. But his father's footprints were not his.

Mack needed to forge his own path. He should be challenged and reminded what it means to take chances and live again. Janie Olsen was just the girl to help him with that. She was smart, sassy and athletic. She would understand his duty to his job came first and foremost because she was definitely low maintenance in that respect. They were perfect for each other. But there was the minor detail of his girlfriend.

"You are beautiful, Christy."

"Aww, you ladies are so sweet and just as lovely, too. I love your little nicknames—Chi Chi and Karmy. Could you please grab my wallet from my purse and dig out the money? I don't want to mess up my new nails."

Karmelle obliged, although with a begrudging frown. "Are you sure about that color? A bright pink polish with a black thumb and ring finger would have added a little bit of sass to your attitude is all I'm saying."

Christy laughed. "This is fine. Thank you."

"Now don't you worry about a thing," said Chimmi as she patted their client on the shoulder. "Karmelle and I will make sure Mack is taken care of at the livestock show."

"I really appreciate you two. I'll bring the trophies and plaques over to the shop then."

Chimmi walked her to the door and waved as she drove away. Turning to face her sister, she said. "That was easier than I thought it would be."

"Now you just have to get Janie there."

"I'll call Belinda at the coffee shop. She's friends with Angie, Janie's sister. Surely we can come up with something."

Karmelle returned to her chair and sunk into it with a plop. "I'm getting rid of this bottle of pale pink polish. Why in the whole of creation would you suggest that color to anyone? It's lifeless. Dull as all git out."

"Not everybody needs to make a statement with their nails. Some people just want a plain manicure."

"There's no reason for that. This town could do with some citizens who want to make a statement. So, tell me, what would a *vessel* be wearing on Saturday to the live-stock show?" Karmelle made little quote marks with her fingers.

"Oh, we're not going. We're just steering Janie there so she can help Mack. If they would spend time together, they'll soon understand how they can't live without each other."

"I am going. I don't want to miss any part of your meddling in other people's lives. And, by the way, stop calling me Karmy. It sounds like 'smarmy', and I don't think that's a good thing."

"Fair enough. Then don't call me Chi Chi."

The sisters grinned and gave each other an air kiss. Chimmi had to admit, her life was much less boring since Karmelle moved to town.

18

JANIE

JANIE FOLLOWED ANGIE THROUGH A MASSIVE sea of pickup trucks and livestock trailers towards a round-top Quonset barn that stood at one end of a grassy parking lot across from the rodeo arena.

The Creek County Fairgrounds had served as the location for stock shows, rodeos, fairs, and traveling revivals for over fifty years. She remembered the spot with full clarity, where the Ferris wheel always sat. It was there, at the base of the ride, her freshman year in high school, she got her first kiss. Roger Lemon.

She knew Roger from science class. He was the pitcher for the Dixon baseball team, ready smile, sharp wit, and she couldn't believe he was even talking to her. His bravery had proved prosperous that night, when he pocketed a hard-earned ten bucks for kissing the ugliest girl in school. Janie had learned of the bet from her sister Angie, and the same week she decided never to give her heart away that easily again. The comments had swirled around her for an entire week, in addition to barking sounds whenever she walked past.

"Ten bucks wasn't enough. Woof. Woof."

"Roger is a good athlete, but he must be dumber than a rock to take that bet."

"Who would wanna kiss that?"

"Her mama must've dropped her on her face."

The laughs and jeers were unending.

She would never tell anyone, but it had been Mack Griffitt who had punched one of the boys who had barked at her. It was during that fallout of humiliation that Janie had also learned that no matter what happened in life, she could always count on her family to speak the truth. Beyond everything else, her brothers and sisters would always have her back.

Janie squared her shoulders against the memory. She wasn't anything like that girl in high school. Definitely smarter, certainly more fit and stronger, and all the wiser. The reality was that she was destined to live life alone, and that was fine by her. She'd made it this far, but now she found herself at another crossroads. A dull and boring existence back in her hometown was not the future she had envisioned for herself.

"Janie! This way." Angie's voice came from two rows of cars over. She jogged to catch up with her sister.

"I'm right behind you."

"Thanks again for helping me out with the trophies," said Angie as she glanced back over her shoulder and gave Janie another once-over from head to toe. "But I wish you had worn something a bit dressier."

This from the sister who was the perfect definition of put-together wherever she went. Everything Angie wore had to coordinate, from the tip of her boots to the top of her hat. And her blonde curls were always in place, her face glowing and ready for a glamor shot. Angie turned heads every time she walked into a room, and Janie had grown up in the shadows, slipping through life unnoticed.

"What is it we're doing? I put on a colored top this time." Janie had thrown on jeans and a tie-dye T-shirt instead of her usual camo wear. And she had dug out a silver buckle with the Rafter O brand and her ostrich Lucchese boots, a Christmas present from several years back.

"You made that shirt at 4-H camp the summer before high school. I have one too, but I would never be caught dead in it now." Angie rolled her eyes. "Don't you have any grown-up clothes? A dress, maybe? Someone might ask you out."

"Why would I wear a dress to the livestock barn?"

"Janie, I told you more than once that we have been asked to help with the awards presentation. It's good publicity for the Rafter O. Dressing appropriately is important."

Janie rolled her eyes. She would never admit it to her sister, but she had put on mascara and lip gloss just on the off chance he might be here. That fire chief interrupted her thoughts day and night, despite how many times she kept telling herself to not think about him. She had relived that Harley ride over and over in her mind many times. She said a silent prayer that he wouldn't be at this event because her cheeks burned every time she remembered that dopey handshake. Shake hands? What an idiot. She couldn't believe she shook his hand. Maybe he was getting ready to kiss her, but the idea made her so nauseous she would have surely hurled her burger right then and there. Not very ladylike.

Seeing as how she never went on any dates, it didn't seem wise to spend her savings on useless things like fancy clothes and makeup. Living at the ranch again with her parents was only temporary until she could figure out where she wanted to be. Janie hated to admit it aloud to her mother, but the mechanic's job for the county had come at the perfect time. She could stash away her paycheck.

"And take that scrunchy out of your hair, for gosh sakes. Since I treated you to a makeover, the least you could do is make an effort to style your hair."

Reluctantly Janie shook out her hair and slipped the band into her jeans pocket. For whatever reason, no one seemed to like her ponytail.

THE OVAL-SHAPED Quonset barn on the fairgrounds was made of corrugated metal and was much larger inside than it looked on the outside. Stifling hot in the summer and freezing in the winter, air circulated through the oversized doors that were left open on both ends.

No surprise that the barn was as crowded as the parking lot. Smells of sweet hay that covered the arena floor mingled with the dust kicked up from trampling two-legged and four-legged stock showgoers.

Janie followed her sister in and around Future Farmers of America kids who stood chatting, some holding on to lead ropes with an assortment of sheep or pigs linked to the other end. Show steers were lined up in the ring, their handlers leading them slowly around in a circle. In the middle, Janie's eyes were drawn immediately to Mack. Drat. Her cheeks burned. Should she ignore him or say hello and shake his hand again? *You are hopeless.* Sometimes, she felt like she had been transported back to junior high school. What was that movie about a mother waking up in her teenager's body?

Her heart thudded. This time he was all Texan. Starched jeans, a bright purple pearl snap shirt, silver belt buckle, and a black Stetson as dark as his ebony hair and mustache. Dark eyes were intently studying the livestock as they passed in front of him. Another man holding a similar clipboard stood at the other end of the arena.

That Mack was certainly an intriguing man. Whether in his fire chief uniform, biker gear, or cowboy boots and jeans, all three personas made her knees wobble. She did not need this kind of distraction in her life right now.

"We made it just in time. The last group is almost done, and then after the scores are tallied, we need to help hand out prizes."

"Why us?"

"You know that the Rafter O sponsors the livestock show every year. Why don't you try and get involved in the community, Janie? You were the exact same way when you lived at home. You have had a lonely existence long enough. It's time you got out into the world. Get involved."

Janie held her tongue and frowned. She had been out in the world, but her sister didn't know about the places she'd traveled to in the military, because no one had even asked her. In fact, since she had been home, her family had not talked about her time in the service. They enjoyed the gifts she had sent from Japan and Germany. But it was almost like they thought she had been away on an extended cruise or vacation, "Janie's Big Adventure." She imagined her mother would have worried if she had been deployed to combat somewhere, and she would have gone wherever the job sent her. But for whatever reason, the Army had her complete her mission in Japan and Germany, learning the trade of mechanics.

Now she was hoping her training would pay off and give her some kind of future.

19
MACK

MACK GRIFFITT KNEW THE MINUTE SHE walked into the barn, despite the fact that he was at the far side studying the backends of a group of swine. Kids followed their entries around the ring, tapping them with a thin stick as they swarmed around Mack. He felt the electricity in the air, and it was all he could do not to look for her in the crowd. He saw her friend's blonde curls and cowboy hat, and he knew Janie wouldn't be far behind. He even turned his back and walked in the opposite direction so he wouldn't be distracted. As if that would stop him from thinking about her. And thinking about her was all he had done these days. From the minute he woke up, her face appeared in his mind, and it was the final image before he drifted to sleep. Even when he and Christy had their weekly set Thursday night date, his thoughts drifted to Janie. And he still didn't even know her last name. Try as he might, he could not remember her from high school.

A snort. A squeal. He turned his attention to the task

at hand as he pointed to two entries. "This young man and this young lady."

The others exited the arena. "After evaluating the top four in the class, I have to go with this young lady on my far left as the winner. I love the toe quality and extra length of body. The balance is good, and he has plenty of presence. This young lady handles her animal very well and needs to be commended." Mack continued assessing the second and third places. "All of the kids have worked real hard and are doing a very good job at getting their animals presented. Let's give them a round of applause as they head back to their pens."

Clapping and whistles echoed through the barn as Mack leaned against the fencing panels to wait on the next group.

"You sure know your pigs." A teasing voice came from behind him. Janie.

"I am a man of many talents." His breath left him for a second as he took in the cowgirl that stood on the other side of the fence rail. Gone was the self-confident air of a soldier.I Instead, the cowboy boots and shiny belt buckle seemed to suit her better.

"Attention in the barn. We have a mom here who has misplaced her daughter. A young lady wearing a yellow T-shirt and pink tennis shoes. If you see her, please bring her to the announcer's stand."

Mack was thankful for the interruption as it gave him a second to catch his breath and gain his composure. His mind blank, he didn't know what to say, but he didn't want her to leave either. The silence hung heavy and awkward between them. She stared at him and he stared back.

Janie spoke first. "I'm going to look for a young lady wearing pink tennis shoes."

Mack nodded and watched her walk away.

One of the parent volunteers walked up to him next. "Do you need anything?"

"At one point, I'm sure I had a clipboard in my hand. Have you seen it?" asked Mack.

"No sir, but I'll look at the announcer's stand."

"Do you know that girl?"

"What girl?"

"The one I was just talking to."

"Janie? Yeah. She's lived here her whole life."

"She has?"

"You don't remember her?"

"Can't say that I do."

The volunteer gave an incredulous look. "Everybody knows Janie. She's back home from the military."

"That's what I hear."

"I'll look for your clipboard."

Mack nodded his head and followed the attendant to the announcer's stand. With everyone engaged in the search, they finally located it in the dirt under the table. Mack bent over to pick it up, stood, and spun around to come face-to-face with Janie again.

True to her word, she was holding the hand of a little girl in pink tennis shoes, tears streaking her cheeks and her bottom lip protruding.

"Milly!" a young woman standing off to one side rushed over and knelt beside the girl, wrapping her in a hug. She looked up. "Thank you, Janie. You're a lifesaver."

Mack studied Janie's face and tried to remember her with darker hair. Maybe it was longer? Maybe she had been chubby in high school? He could not remember any classmate by the name of Janie. It bugged him that there was something familiar about her. Or maybe he just wanted there to be.

She patted the child on the shoulder, nodded her head, and turned to leave.

"Where did you find her?" asked Mack.

"Walking through the rabbit cages. That's where I would have been at her age." She smiled, her eyes shiny and bright.

Mack couldn't think of anything to say in return. He stood there like an utter fool staring at her, not wanting her to leave but too proud to ask her to stay near. He sighed and sat down.

During the rest of the afternoon, Mack searched for Janie. He watched her eat a hot dog. She cleared tables and carried out the trash. At one point, she actively stopped a runaway goat by blocking his path and grabbing him around the neck. That made Mack laugh out loud. Finally, after groups of swine, goats, and heifers, it was time to hand out ribbons and trophies. Chimmi and Karmelle appeared carrying boxes.

"Where's Christy?" he asked. The chamber's involvement was a big deal every year, and Christy always assisted him with the awards.

"We found someone else to help. Christy had a meeting." Chimmi smiled.

About that time, Angie appeared with Janie, who wore a surprised look on her face as Chimmi and Karmelle ushered her towards the stage.

"Where is my assistant?" Mack asked.

Angie nudged Janie forward. "She's right here."

"Wait. I'm helping him?" Janie asked.

With Christy's usual efficiency, everything was neat and orderly in the box and someone shoved a winner's list into his hand.

Mack pointed to the box. "Figure out which prize goes with which kid. I'll call the names out and you hand me the right ribbon."

"I can do that." Janie said.

Mack had never enjoyed anything more, and seeing the smiles on the kids' faces was always rewarding. This was one of his favorite events of the year. Having Janie by his side made it even better. They hardly spoke, but she was so calming and gave every kid a hug as they came forward to get their award. Janie wasn't bubbly or hyper, and she did not grab the microphone from him the way Christy always did. Instead, they seemed to work in sync and almost had a mental telepathy. And once, Mack caught Janie looking at him, from his head to his hands to his boots, and then she quickly turned away.

He only had two more awards to go when Christy suddenly appeared at the edge of the stage.

"I see you found someone to help you." Her cheeks were flushed, and a fake smile formed on her mouth but did not reach her eyes. Christy fanned her face with a paper from her stylish purse.

"Am I in your way?" Janie asked, a look of confusion on her face.

"You're doing great!" Chimmi said. Karmelle stood on one side of her and Angie was on the other, all three of them beaming up at Janie. Coffee shop Belinda walked up to join the group as well.

"Hand me the microphone, Mack." Instead of waiting, Christy joined him on the stage and tapped the end of the mic with her finger. "Thanks again, everyone, for joining us. And congratulations to the winners. Y'all have worked so hard and it shows."

Janie glared at all of them, looking from one to the other. She spun on her heel and walked off the stage ignoring her friends. Mack watched until she disappeared out the door at the far end.

"Oh," piped up Christy as she covered one end of the mic with her hand. "I guess your helper left." She shrugged her shoulders. The remainder of the day wasn't nearly as fun, and Mack worried about what he might have done or said. He looked for Janie but never saw her come back to the building.

JANIE

"You betrayed me." Janie barely waited for Angie to climb into the truck and shut the door.

"How do you figure?"

"You set me up to be on that stage with Mack. You all did."

"What are you talking about?"

"I saw you standing there with Chimmi, Karmelle, and Belinda." Tears started to well up in Janie's eyes, angry tears. She fought against them. But all those times in school when she was made fun of, called names, and singled out for being different flooded into her mind. Why couldn't people just leave her alone?

"There was no conspiracy against you. Mack needed someone to help him hand out awards."

"Why me? How did my name come up?"

"I don't remember. You weren't doing anything, were you?" Angie let out a big puff of air.

"That's not the point."

"Why couldn't you help him then?"

"I feel like I'm some pity case that the whole town is working on."

"You're too sensitive, Janie. That's ridiculous."

"Ugly little Plain Jane needs help finding a man, so why not throw her up against the most handsome man in the county? You are all a bunch of meddling do-gooders, and I'm not going to be a part of it."

Janie fumed as silence permeated the pickup cab.

"I never said Mack Griffitt was the most handsome man in the county," Angie said in a calm, soft murmur. Her lips curved upwards in a playful grin.

"What?"

"No one ever mentioned how good-looking the fire chief is." Her voice tinged with humor, which only made Janie angrier. Her cheeks reddened.

"Well, that's what you're doing." Janie stopped her lip from forming a pout.

"We are not meddling, and besides, there are other single guys in the county. The sheriff deputy, for instance."

"Sure. See if you can get me a ride-along. Why not start taking names, and let's inject me into the lives of every eligible bachelor in town. Surely one of them is so desperate he might take pity on me and be my boyfriend."

"Janie. You are not ugly. Don't say that."

"Don't patronize me. You're my sister. You, of all people, should shoot straight. I always thought I could trust you, Angie."

"Which is why I'm saying that you are not ugly. Since you came back home, you are more fit than I've seen you in your entire life. You have a glow about you that wasn't there before. You seem smarter and more self-assured. I wish I had half of your self-confidence."

"I am in shape. That's one thing the Army did for me."

"And that haircut and color just added gravy to the biscuit, thanks to me."

"Okay, I agree. I do like my hair, but I wish that you would accept me for what I am and stop trying to fix me up with men. I'm not pretty. I'm dull and boring. No one wants a dull-looking girlfriend. I understand that, and I'm okay with living my life alone."

"So now you're comparing yourself to some show heifer? You can believe what you want, but I believe that God has someone for all of us, and you just haven't met your person yet. And if I were a bettin' gal, I'd put my money on the fire chief."

Janie was surprised at that comment, which stunned her into silence. Her heart skipped a beat and she hesitated several minutes before replying.

"It seems to me that you don't need anyone's help. You and Mack keep running into each other. Maybe he has something to do with it. You should blame him, not your friends."

"What are you talking about?" Janie was confused. She almost felt like crying, but she held any emotion in. Maybe it was anger. Or that old feeling of being the tomboy, the ugly one the boys made fun of.

"The way Mack Griffitt looks at you. That man is smitten. I'd bet the Rafter O on it."

That was the most ridiculous thing she had ever heard. She squinted her eyes.

"He has a girlfriend. Christy from the chamber." Janie said with a roll of her eyes. "He told me so."

"When did you and Mack discuss Christy?"

"The other day after work."

"After work when?" Angie pulled one leg up in the seat and turned to face her sister.

"He pulled up on his Harley and asked me if I wanted to go for a ride. I might have asked about his girlfriend."

Angie yelled, "What? You never told me any of this. So, what'd he say?"

Janie hunkered down into the seat, bowed her head, and closed her eyes. Here we go.

"She doesn't like his bike."

"And then what happened?"

Janie paused. There was no easy answer to deflect Angie's questioning now. She was hot on the trail of something, and she knew it. Janie considered how to make this long story short and then change the subject.

"I went for a ride, and then we ate burgers."

"What?" Angie's eyes were bugged. "Where?"

"Does it matter?"

"Yes. Where'd you go?"

"If you must know, he drove out to Palo Duro Canyon and then we stopped at a burger joint on Route 66 on the way back."

"Wait a minute. This was after work?"

"Yes." Angie turned the key in the ignition. "Can we go home now?"

Angie nodded.

"So, let me get this straight. He picked you up after work, in the evening. And then you drove all the way to the canyon." Angie sat in silence for a minute and then punched Janie on the arm. "Mack took you to watch a sunset in Palo Duro Canyon! Did he kiss you?"

"Heavens, no." Janie shook her head vigorously. "Stop looking at me like that. He did not kiss me. And if he did, I wouldn't tell you."

"That is breaking the sisterhood code, a code that has

been around for a millennium. You have to tell me every detail."

"First of all, there is no such thing as a sisterhood code, and second of all, I don't think you know what millennium even means."

Anger clouded Angie's eyes for a brief second, and then she smiled. "I know what you're doing. Trying to get me riled over something else to distract me from the topic at hand, which is the fact that the fire chief likes you."

"He was glad to see Christy today. He is not even the slightest bit interested in me."

Angie put the pickup in gear and slowly backed out of the parking space. Her sister had grown silent for the time being, which might be a sign of trouble. Only time would tell.

Very obvious from the way Mack acted today when she arrived at the stock show, the first thing he asked about was Christy. There was no way she would ever attract the attention of someone like Mack, so why did her heart skip a beat again, and why did she keep remembering their bike ride over and over?

Angie made a spitting sound, a raspberry, with her tongue, just like when they were kids sharing a bedroom. "Mack and Christy have had a standing date every Thursday night. She's safe for him. No commitment. No effort because she'll always be there. But that's not going to satisfy him forever. He needs someone who will shake up his world. Get him out of his rut. *You* are the girl to do that, Janie. Now you just have to believe it."

"I am not interested in being someone's therapist or their good time."

"We think he likes you."

"We? How many are involved in this crazy romance

A FIERY MATCH

plan?" Janie held up her hand. "No. Don't tell me. I don't want to know."

Janie crossed her arms across her chest and set her lips to a thin line. She was not contributing to this conversation another minute. Mack and Christy's relationship was none of her business.

Clearly, everyone in Dixon was delusional. The sooner she got out of this town and started her new life, the better. If she just had someplace to go.

21

JANIE

Janie groaned at the buzz. Two o'clock. The mayor had insisted that she add the county's emergency app to her phone so that she would be alerted if there were any law enforcement or fire business. The text read, "9-1-1 emergency. Propane tank on fire. Henderson Farm." The first thing that came to mind was rain. It had started just before dark that night, and as all country folk know, rain means mud, and mud means impassable dirt roads. The heavy fire trucks would never make it through. She swung her legs over the edge of her bed and rubbed her eyes.

They would need the backhoe. If she were a betting girl, she would bet those trucks would slide right into the ditch and never make it to Henderson's place. She dug for some pants out of the dirty clothes basket, tugged on her boots, and looked for a raincoat in the mud room, but they were all gone.

Four-wheel drive would get her to the Hendersons' place with no problem. Their farm wasn't far, if she stayed on the back roads bypassing the main highway and circling north of town. She could be there in fifteen minutes tops.

Outside, the chill in the air tingled her nose. She took a deep breath of the cleansing rain as she hurried to her truck to find a leather jacket, ball cap, and gloves. Fat drops pinged her back, causing a chill to run down her spine. The keys were there and the engine started with a roar, breaking the silence of the early morning calm. Everyone was probably awake now, but there was no other way. Flipping the switch to four-wheel drive, she fishtailed when her tires hit the slick dirt road. She turned into the spin and gunned it again, headlights illuminating slashes of rain and a puddled road.

THE DIRT ROAD to the Henderson farm had turned into a gooier mess than the Rafter O ranch road had been. Janie struggled to keep the truck in the center. She made a sharp left turn and had to stop to unlatch the gate. The rain wasn't going to give them a break. The farmhouse was lit up like a Christmas tree, every window shone yellow, and porch lights brightened the veranda that circled three sides of the house. She could not see any flames. The propane tank must be at the back of the house. She slowly drove through the front and circled around in that direction.

Her heart took a leap and, without thinking, she jumped out of the truck in one fluid motion and rushed closer. A flame flickering three to four feet high burned at one end of the tank. As she got closer, she noticed the source of the fire was the hose that came from the ground and not the tank itself. Mr. Henderson was standing nearby with a garden hose, squirting a low stream of water from side to side in a casual manner, as though he was watering his tomatoes.

"What happened?"

"There was an explosion. Sure did rock the house and break our bathroom window." Mr. Henderson never turned to look at her, but stood stone still, fixated on the flames as he directed the hose.

Janie almost did not see the woman kneeling at the edge of their backyard, but she heard her first. "Lord, we praise you. Take us up into the air with you. We're ready to go."

"What's wrong with your wife?" asked Janie as she hurried over to her. "Is she hurt?"

"Mama thinks it's the Rapture. She was reading her Bible just before bedtime and the explosion that woke us up convinced her this was it."

"What's it?"

"She thinks it's the end of times. I just wanna put this fire out before Jesus calls me home."

"Thank goodness it's raining, otherwise the entire pasture would be burning right now." She turned to Mrs. Henderson. "Ma'am, would you like to go back inside and get out of this rain?"

"Not leaving," the old woman said.

Janie's stomach clenched. Keeping the propane tank cool was definitely the thing to do, but she had doubts about the pathetic stream of water coming from the garden hose. She had no idea how to handle a scared woman. She turned to watch Farmer Henderson, then back to his wife, not really knowing which way to direct her attention. Maybe they should all evacuate?

"What should we do?" Farmer Henderson asked the question calmly, like they were sitting in the local coffee shop and he had just asked her if she wanted a muffin or a doughnut.

"I think you're doing great. Keeping the tank cool is good. The fire department should be here anytime. Do you have a wrench somewhere?"

"Yeah. Out in the tool shed," he pointed.

"We should probably shut off the valve, if I can get close enough."

Suddenly Mr. Henderson dropped the hose. "I'll turn off the lights. Maybe we shouldn't be using electricity?"

Janie couldn't think of a reasonable argument, so she left him to his mission and turned her attention to the shed to find a crescent wrench. Using her cell phone for light, she mumbled to herself over forgetting the flashlight that was still in her car back at the Rafter O. She hunched her shoulders against the rain and slogged through the mud.

"Where is your tractor, Mr. Henderson?" She called back to him. "They may need it in case the fire trucks get stuck."

"She's parked inside the main barn, but you may have to charge the battery."

"Okay, thanks." She jogged up the hill towards the small shed that loomed just on the edge of the back porch light and then remembered she should have driven her truck in case they needed to hook up to the tractor. What a night. And where was the fire department?

22
MACK

MACK PULLED INTO THE FIRE STATION AND glanced at the screen that pinpointed the location of the 9-1-1 emergency. They didn't need a map though. His volunteers were all local men, and they knew where the Henderson farm was located. Mack quickly and efficiently assigned one guy to drive the engine and one guy to drive the tanker with water. He assigned others to ride on specific trucks, and in record time, they had on their gear and pulled out in front of him, sirens blaring.

Both fire trucks shattered the early morning silence. Mack was certainly worried about the Hendersons, but he couldn't help but feel a sense of pride every time those shiny trucks rolled out of their garage. He had a capable crew too. Each and every one of them were skilled and dedicated to their purpose.

They didn't have to worry about traffic, sailing through the midtown four-way stop sign at Main Street and Main Avenue without stopping. The town of Dixon rolled up the streets by eight o'clock on weeknights.

They headed east out of town, sirens screaming.

Mack figured they could make good time by staying on the blacktop, and then it was a short drive to the farm with only a mile of dirt road.

From the light of his truck, he could see the mud churning and rolling under the heavy vehicles in front of him, as the tires made deep trenches on the road. They moved at a snail's pace, the back end of the truck fish-tailing and coming back to center as the driver struggled with the equipment. Mack couldn't tell how the first truck was doing. The clouds blocked the night stars and moon. He was surrounded by a blackness that afforded no hint of what was outside the ring of light cast by his truck lights. As long as they kept moving, they should make it fine. But then the fire engine's brake lights pierced the rain and dark, and the truck came to a stop.

The driver opened his door and stuck his head out, looking back. Mack rolled his window down and leaned out.

"We're both stuck," he yelled.

Mack gritted his teeth and stepped out of the warm pickup into the rain. As he walked around the fire engine, he could see the first one in line was bogged down too, but it was worse. They had slid off the road into the ditch at an angle blocking the entire route.

They'd need to call for a backhoe to pull these trucks out, and someone needed to get to the Henderson's farm to assess the situation. Normally they would call Big Jim at the county shop, and he would load the backhoe on the trailer and come to their aid. But he didn't have Janie's number, and she would be of no use to them in this situation anyway.

"Farmer Henderson probably has a tractor." The volunteers had gathered in the middle of the road between the two fire engines.

"I don't think it's big enough to pull these trucks," another said.

"We need the maintainer."

They turned to see the lights of another vehicle slow to a stop behind the chief's pickup. Deputy Skinner emerged and walked their way.

"You guys stuck?" He let out a long, low whistle. "You're in a mighty fine pickle, looks like to me."

No one commented on his statement of the obvious.

"I'll call Janie," the deputy said. "She can bring the backhoe or maintainer."

Mack shook his head. "No. She can't help us, and she can't load that equipment on a trailer by herself."

"Sure, she can." The deputy punched in a number.

Mack frowned. It annoyed him that the deputy had shown up, it annoyed him that Jack was ignoring Mack's instruction, and it was even more annoying that he had Janie's phone number.

"She's not answering. I'll keep trying." He slipped his phone back into the front pocket of his jacket.

"I'll go on to the house and check the situation. We can't forget about why we're here in the first place," Mack said. "You guys work to get that truck out of the ditch, or maybe the other one can get by and drive on to the Hendersons."

"Will do, Chief."

THE RAIN HAD CHANGED to a fine mis,t but an occasional drip continued to fall from his helmet. He cautiously worked at staying in the center of the road, his flashlight casting a bouncing pool of light on muddy puddles with standing water and more mud. If his memory was correct, he only had about half a mile to walk before he reached the gate that led into their farm.

In the dark, it was difficult to determine how far he was from the farmhouse. He saw no light. Mesquite trees grew thick behind the barbed wire on either side of the road. As he trudged along, he gritted his teeth and pondered the options. He needed to get those trucks moving, and the closest solution would be using Henderson's tractor. Without Big Jim, he couldn't think of any other way to drag them to the house.

Why didn't he have Janie's number? He had a call roster for every other city and county employee, and as fire chief, he was furnished with an updated list. She wasn't listed. He still didn't even know her last name.

His calculations were right. In about half a mile, he came to a metal gate that already stood open. Crossing the cattle guard, he skirted a deep pool of muddy water by walking around it on the grass. He could see a faint light at the barns and one at the corral, but the house stood dark and looming, barely visible through the trees. As he made his way cautiously towards the structure, all of his senses were alert. He couldn't smell smoke. Thank goodness for the rain. He rounded the corner of the house. On the far side of the property, he saw the live flames, jumping and flickering at one end of the propane tank.

Mack's legs went into action without a second thought. By the time he was halfway across the yard, the flames suddenly disappeared. A figure stood up, holding a crescent wrench over her head.

"I did it!" she yelled.

Mack froze in place. How had she gotten here so quickly?

Janie dropped the wrench and rushed over to the edge

of the patio, where she wrapped a purple sleeping bag tighter around Mrs. Henderson and her chair, covering her in a warm, waterproof cocoon.

"Coffee's ready. Would you like some, Chief?" Mr. Henderson stood in the doorway, propping the screen door open with an elbow and holding a mug of steaming liquid out in front of him.

He shook his head no to the offer from Henderson.

Janie started and looked up. The look of relief that came over her face made his chest tighten. She smiled broadly and stood firm.

A smile just for him.

Meant only for him.

Under the light of a single lightbulb, a look of relief passed over her face, and she nodded and took a few steps closer to him. He ran his eyes over her. Petite legs ended in a pair of biker boots that looked a size too big. She stuffed both hands into a black leather bomber jacket and pushed back the olive-green ball cap with the word ARMY emblazoned across the front.

They both stood frozen in time, watching and waiting. Waiting for what, he did not know.

The only words that came from his mouth were, "Where is the tractor?" Any other words were lost because his brain had shut down at the sight of her.

He wanted to rage at her for standing next to an open flame like that. He wanted to tell her he was glad to see her too.

He wanted to see that smile again.

23

MACK

MACK WATCHED JANIE HESITATE AND BLINK with confusion as if she wasn't sure he was really standing there at the Henderson farm. "What did you say?" she asked.

"I need the tractor."

Chief Mack walked towards the patio where Janie stood next to Mrs. Henderson. Mr. Henderson handed a mug of coffee to his wife and disappeared back inside. He quickly came back with another mug and took a sip.

"Sure thing, Chief. It's parked in the large barn. Janie already has the battery charging. She figured you'd need it."

Janie looked at him with a look of irritation. What did she think he should be doing? Sit down for a friendly cup of coffee? He had both fire engines stuck, his entire department was currently huddled in the middle of a muddy road at three o'clock in the morning, and he was doing the best he could with what he had.

From his canvas coat, he pulled a flashlight out again.

"It's this way," Janie said.

They walked across the gravel drive side by side towards the barn. He illuminated their path with his flashlight. Mack climbed up into the tractor and turned the ignition. Nothing.

An overhead light suddenly came on. She took her hand off the switch, looked at him and shrugged. "Might as well light the place up, don't you think?"

She had used Henderson's truck and attached jumper cables to the tractor. She eased into the pickup truck and revved the engine several times. Mack tried to start it again. Nothing.

"How long has it been hooked up?" he asked.

"About half an hour. You might as well come back to the house and drink that coffee Mr. Henderson made for you. We should have a charge in another thirty minutes."

Reluctantly he knew she was right, but he didn't have to tell her so. He climbed out of the tractor, she jumped to the ground from the truck, and they walked back towards the house. His long legs ate up the ground in determined, steady strides, and she jogged to stay up with him.

He gave the crew an update with a quick text.

In the light of the kitchen, she looked even more beautiful. Her cheeks were flushed from the walk, and her face was moist with rain. Her hair hung in damp rivulets down the back of her leather coat. She stood with legs apart, hands on hips, and gone was that sweet look of relief from earlier. In its place was a steely-eyed glare as though she was about to serve his head on a platter.

He watched her with caution, took a sip of coffee, and prepared himself for anything. A woman could get riled over the slightest thing and strike without warning.

"Aren't you going to ask him about his fire?" Janie's voice cut the air like a sharp razor.

Mack choked on his coffee. "Oh, yes." He coughed again. "Mr. Henderson, we need to check out that propane tank."

"Janie put the fire out already."

"Yes, sir. I saw that." He ignored her. They would definitely be discussing the incident in full at another time. He set his mug on the table and hurried back outside.

Janie appeared at his side and took the flashlight from his hand. One arm and shoulder grew warm from her heat. She smelled of rain and coconut shampoo. He tried to focus, but it wasn't easy. Her lips, and how they might feel against his, danced in his head.

Only through self-imposed will did he note the blackened ground. The pipe leading from the ground to one end of the tank was charred, but in the dark, he couldn't tell the extent of the damage. He placed a hand on the tank.

"Hold the light higher." he said. "This is the valve that shuts it off to the house, and this is the valve that shuts off the propane from the ground. You turned the wrong one, but the tank is cool."

"I just had her filled about a week ago." Henderson offered.

"That's why it didn't explode then. The full tank stayed cool, and the wet grass kept it from spreading and burning half the county."

They all walked back to the barn, and Mack explained the situation about the fire engines, still sitting in the middle of the road.

"I didn't know you had both of your trucks stuck, Chief. You should have said something. This old tractor won't do ya no good. You can use Agnes. She's parked on the other side of the barn."

Mack and Janie looked at each other with a questioning glance and followed the old man past the barn and around the other side to discover another set of double doors. Henderson swung them open and he disappeared into the dark, his flashlight dancing on the dirt floor. A door clicked, a grunt, and then a roar of an engine. Lights as bright as a football field pierced the darkness and made Mack squint. Henderson emerged from his barn driving a backhoe.

Mack wanted to shout with glee.

Janie doubled over with a snort, and then let out a deep belly laugh. She stopped laughing and walked closer when Henderson pulled to a stop.

"I'm driving," she said.

The temporary county mechanic was not in charge of this fire scene, and he would not be taking orders from her. He was the Chief. He gave the orders.

"No. You're not." Mack said.

24
JANIE

JANIE COULDN'T TAKE HER EYES OFF THE FIRE chief. He was such an imposing figure, particularly when he was in his element, but she was going to drive Mr. Henderson's backhoe, and there wasn't any other scenario that was going to work.

Mack suddenly turned his attention to her and slowly ambled her way. The air left her lungs, and her heart took a leap, but she worked at keeping the look on her face neutral despite what was going on inside.

"You are not driving that piece of equipment."

She squared off in front of him, not eye to eye because he was a whole foot taller than her, but she held her own. "Yes, I am. You know I can do it. Let's get going."

Mr. Henderson now stood on the ground between them, looking at one, then the other. Janie walked around him and climbed up in the cab.

"Well, are you coming?" She held the door open, waiting for Mack to make a move. "I'll give you a ride, if you hurry."

His face turned red, and she could see his jaw clench in the lights from the backhoe. She gave him a sweet smile. "You're not winning this argument, Chief. You might as well climb in."

He stepped up on the ladder. "This isn't going to happen. You are not a trained volunteer. We can't do this."

"Sure we can. I'll scoot to one side and we can share the seat. It's big enough. In fact, I'll let you drive us down the road." She couldn't help but wonder if his comment held a double meaning. Was he only talking about her driving, or did he think she was making a move on him? Not if he were the last male on the face of the earth. No, thank you.

He raised the bucket and engaged the gears, and tingles ran up her thigh when his leg pressed against it. They were cozy, that was for certain. She sat sideways, failing to find the best place for her arm, and finally stretched it around behind him. Her heart thudded, but she told herself it was just adrenaline from the excitement of the night. Actually, it was early morning now. She tried to ignore the smell of him. All male. Sweat mixed with the musky dampness on his fire gear. He suddenly turned and peered at her from under the bill of the helmet.

"How did you get here so fast?" They chugged along towards the gate, driving straight through the puddle that stood at the entrance.

"The mayor hooked me up to the app."

"But how did you know to charge the tractor?"

"I grew up living in the country, and with all the rain we've had this evening, I knew your trucks would have a time of it on these roads."

"Which way did you come?"

"Don't they say the fastest distance between two points is a straight line? So instead of going around by following the blacktop, I stayed on the county road out of town that headed straight on FM 295."

He studied her for a minute, but she couldn't read him. Was he angry? Disappointed?

"Are you happy with how things went tonight?" she cautiously asked, trying to determine his mood.

He shrugged and kept driving the equipment towards his men.

The fire department still occupied the middle of the road, making no headway to dislodge the trucks. What a mess they had made of the road and ditch. Janie didn't try to hide the giggle that bubbled up from her throat. It could have been a lot worse. Mack climbed out of the cab and hopped to the ground.

Looking up at her, he said, "Get down." and motioned for her to move.

She slid over to the middle of the seat, leaning closer to reach the door handle, and said, "No, sir."

She slammed the door closed in his face. The moment she did it, she regretted her action because if looks could kill, she would definitely be greeting St. Peter at the gate this very second. Sitting close together in the cab, they had reached some sort of a truce, but now she had undone any common ground they might have.

Regrettably, Janie had won that argument without much of a fight, but she wondered if it would be as easy the next time they disagreed about something. She wasn't so sure that he was familiar with being around a strong-willed woman. Christy didn't seem to be that way at all. She was so much nicer and accommodating. Janie didn't have time to be nice. She had a job to do.

The men looped a chain between the two pieces of

equipment and she expertly eased the first truck out of the ditch, backing up for several hundred feet. They unlooped the pull chain, and she eased around the fire truck, having to drop her tires into the muddy ditch that was churned up from the truck tires. She made it around and headed towards the second truck. It was a slow process, but she was successful at pulling that one out too.

The rain had stopped, but the water stood in low places on the road, making the mud a soupy mess. She would have to pull the trucks the entire half-mile to the Hendersons' place, and that is what she did. They attached the chain again, she pulled the first one the half-mile to the farmhouse, and went back for the tanker truck.

With both trucks in his driveway, Mr. Henderson stood in his yard, but his wife was not with him. Janie wondered how he had talked her into going into the house. The men spilled out and surrounded the propane tank, looking and discussing. Two of them went inside the house and two others walked the perimeter of the yard. By now, the sky held the first rays of light.

Farmer Henderson opened the back door. "Want some coffee? Mabel has some cinnamon buns too, hot from the oven."

"Now you're talking." The chief laughed and, without another word to his men, followed the farmer inside. The volunteers seemed unconcerned about the propane tank at this point, so they followed their chief inside as well.

Janie stood there alone and stunned. That's it? The very spot where live flames had flared next to a tank full of fuel now seemed of little concern. Before she could follow, Deputy Skinner came outside and handed her a mug with a bun on a napkin.

"Thought you could use something."

She looked at him in surprise. "Thank you, Jack. How nice. I didn't realize you were here."

He grinned, thinking her gratitude meant for him to keep standing next to her. Now it just got weird, but she took a bite of the buttery bread anyway.

"This is delicious," she said as she munched.

He chuckled. "Mrs. Henderson makes the best in the county. She sells them at the fair every year."

"I remember the county fair, but I don't recall ever seeing Mrs. Henderson's buns there." She giggled. "You know what I mean."

Deputy Jack's face went scarlet and he fidgeted, then took several sips of coffee. She could feel his stare. This could not be good.

"About Saturday," he said. "Want to go to a movie?"

A movie with the deputy. She hadn't been to a movie in a decade, so why not? He had her at a weak moment, standing there idle with food in her mouth.

"Sure." she said before stuffing the rest of the sticky bun in her mouth so she wouldn't have to continue the conversation.

"I'll text you the time."

She nodded and watched him saunter to his cruiser. From inside the Hendersons' house, she could hear the men laughing, interrupted by the occasional deep voice of their chief. She sighed. The heart never gets what it wants in her case. Why did she care anyway? The man was infuriating.

25
MACK

As the fire department volunteers arrived for the Thursday morning staff meeting, Mack's thoughts were on Janie, not the business at hand. Part of him was still irritated. What a stubborn, pig-headed woman she was. He'd never known anyone like her. Admittedly, for a girl, she had skills. She could sure make that machinery do what she wanted, but he would never tell her that.

As if the entire universe was against him, he glanced up and there she was. Standing just inside the door, gazing around the room.

"What are *you* doing here?" Not the friendliest greeting, but it escaped from his mouth before he could stop it. Her cheeks flushed and a hurtful look passed over her face, which she stifled within seconds. That made him feel even worse.

"I invited her," Deputy Jack said. "She was the first one on scene at the Henderson farm."

Janie ignored the chief and eased into a chair next to the deputy. He gave her a warm smile. A few of the other men offered their greetings.

"Hello, Janie."

"If I'm ever stuck again, you're on my speed dial."

She laughed. "Maybe you should learn how to drive in the mud."

Mack was surprised at how comfortable she fit in with the guys, almost like one of the volunteers herself. Deputy Jack leaned back in his chair and extended his arm across the back of Janie's chair. Irritation spread through Mack like a wildfire, as if the deputy had some claim on her. It was an inappropriate gesture for a professional setting, in Mack's opinion. They had business to discuss. This wasn't the local pizzeria.

Everyone settled, and Mack rapped on the table. "Let's make this assessment quick. I have a budget to work on before next week's City Council meeting. We have several items to discuss."

He stood at the front of the room, half sitting and half leaning against a table. He began with a review of safety protocols for grass fires, equipment maintenance, and cleaning instructions for maintaining their uniforms. He usually wasn't this thorough, but maybe Janie's presence irritated him.

Equipment checks were next, with everything seeming to be in working order. Each volunteer was responsible for cleaning their own gear.

"And now let's talk about propane tank safety and the 9-1-1 call to the Henderson farm. Unfortunately, the first on scene was not properly trained in this safety procedure, and hence, the wrong valve was turned off."

He could have heard a pin drop, as the room grew strangely quiet.

"An explosion did not occur, thank God, and all went fairly smoothly after we got unstuck. Once again, we sorely missed Big Jim. Mr. Henderson's backhoe served us well. I need someone to run out there and double-check everything."

"I can," a young man held up his hand. "My wife talked to Mrs. Henderson yesterday and their hot water heaters had to be reignited, their internet is back working, and they're doing all right."

"Thanks for that update." Chief Mack looked down at his notes.

He happened to glance up and noticed flushed cheeks and gritted teeth as Janie watched him. Good. She was mad at him again. Nothing new there. Hopefully, she would leave right after the meeting.

The morning meeting went by quickly. As each volunteer reported on the calls they had been involved in the week before, Mack made a few notes. As they ambled towards the door after the meeting, he couldn't help but overhear the deputy.

"I'll see you Saturday, then?" Deputy Jack asked Janie. She smiled, nodded, and, before leaving the room, shot Mack a glaring glance without saying another word to anyone else.

Mack shrugged off her obvious anger, walked through the fire station to his office, and turned his attention to the budget spreadsheet that he needed to finish. Digging around on his desk, he found the yellow pad with notes of needed items.

The clearing of a throat interrupted his thoughts. He looked up. Janie stood in the doorway with arms crossed over her chest, leaning against the door facing. Her usual biker boots crossed at the ankle, tight jeans, another Army-issue green T-shirt, and her hair pulled back in a tight ponytail.

"I'm really busy right now. Can this wait?" Even to

him, his voice was obviously curt and rude. He had no idea why he was acting this way.

"Why do you hate me?" Unlike most women, she had no tears in her eyes when she asked the question. Her voice was calm, like she was asking if he wanted another helping of mashed potatoes. He didn't hate her. Far from it.

"What is this, junior high?" He really did not have time to go into this right now. Unexpectedly, his question made her laugh.

"I can see you're busy, but I wanted you to know that I have been fully trained in firefighting. Fighting fires, handling hazardous material, treating people with smoke inhalation."

"We don't have any job openings at this time, but I appreciate your skills." That came out a little sarcastic, even to his ears.

She ignored him and continued. "That's not to say your men don't know what they're doing, it's just that my training was geared more toward the explosives type situation. As far as propane tanks, every valve and hose can be set up differently, and in the dark, it's next to impossible to understand the plumbing and know for certain what I did was right."

He opened his mouth to reply, but she held up her hand as she walked closer to his desk. He ignored the gesture. "Why didn't you provide this information during the meeting?" he asked before she could continue.

"True, I should have waited for someone else to get there, but once I got the fire turned off, Mrs. Henderson seemed to calm down more. She truly thought the world was ending." She stood right in front of his desk by now and leaned closer to meet him eye to eye.

"As far as my abilities, if you ever chastise me in front of your entire department again in that tone of voice, I will hurt you in ways you never thought possible. Is that clear?"

Oh, she was angry, all right. Angier than he had ever seen a woman before. Her eyes burned a hole through his, and her hands were clenched so tight on top of his desk, her knuckles were white. Words were lost to him at the nearness of her face. He had acted horribly, there was no doubt, but she irritated him like no other woman had ever done before.

"You're right. I do owe you an apology."

Surprise washed over her face, and for once, she was speechless. He took a little pride in knowing that. They stared without blinking, until his gaze dropped to her lips. So close, and with a little effort, he could claim them.

"Let's call a truce," he said. "It's obvious you're here to stay until Big Jim gets back, so I will agree to get along if you'll agree that I run my department and I give the orders. No exceptions."

"Okay," she squeaked and cleared her throat. "I agree. A truce."

Where was the fireball from only minutes before? He had to stifle a laugh. "Let's get you some bunker gear in case we need your services again."

"Okay," she said again, her mouth agape in surprise.

"Come this way. I know I have a small-sized fire suit, but you may need extra-small. I'll assign you a locker too."

She followed him into the garage in complete silence. He wanted to make a comment on how quiet she had suddenly become, but decided against it. He helped her step into the pants which had liners, and just as he figured, the straps were way too long, so he stepped closer.

"Turn around." he said as he spun her around to adjust the straps on the back. He held the jacket up so she could slip her arms inside. He spun her back around to face him.

"Let me see." The coat was a size too big, and he couldn't help but stare. Her eyes were wide, still surprised, and maybe a bit untrusting. She stood perfectly still, in a big yellow coat with reflective tape, her hands all but hidden in the sleeves, and the pant bottoms pooled around those biker boots. There wasn't anything else for him to do but lean closer and kiss her.

Instinctively her lips parted, and he became lost in the soft sensation. Mack came up for air and noticed her parted lips, wide eyes, and flushed face. She raised up on her tiptoes and found his lips again. With a deep sigh, she wrapped both arms around his neck. He pulled her closer, slightly lifting her feet off the ground. He broke the spell, and then he did something even more horrible. On wobbly legs, he took three steps back.

Mixed emotions ran across her face, from shock to anger, and then her eyes clouded with hurt. A look so sad and broken, he would never forget it.

She shrugged the coat off, stepped out of the fire department overalls, and left. Within minutes the door to the fire station slammed in response, matching the slamming of his heart in his chest.

Boy, did he mess that up, but he had not been prepared for the effect that kiss had on him. It rocked him to his core, and there was no going back now.

26

JANIE

JANIE WALKED WITH PURPOSE THE TWO BLOCKS from the fire station to the county mechanic's shop, not even looking when she crossed the street. Her lips burned, and her face did too, with humiliation. What had possessed him to do something like that? And what made her even madder was the fact that she never saw it coming. Not in a million years. And, it was nice. Worse than all that, she had opened her mouth and kissed him back.

She hurried inside the shop and began putting away tools, getting things ready to close up for the day. A horn honked and she glanced outside the open garage door to see her sister pull up and park. Angie stuck her head out the window.

"Hurry up. I made an appointment for nails and toes at Chimmi's."

Janie cringed. She did not feel like hanging around a bunch of cackling women. Not now, with her heart still beating like thunder in her chest. She didn't know whether to laugh hysterically or start sobbing. Either way, her sister Angie would harass the devil out of her for the details. Janie didn't feel like talking about it. That's the last thing she wanted to do.

The thought of going home to sit alone in her childhood room sounded even worse. Been there and done that before. *Get a life, Janie, for goodness sake.*

Nails and toes it is then. She sighed and nodded at her sister. In the bathroom, she scrubbed her fingernails and hands with Lava soap, and even used a nail brush. They looked halfway better. She pulled down both garage doors, and stepped out of the office, turning to lock the door behind her.

"Let the torture begin," she said to Angie as she climbed into the ranch pickup truck.

Her sister laughed. Angie looked perfectly put together, like always, and the last place she needed was a beauty shop. Her hair hung straight and shiny today, without curls, a red collared embroidered shirt with the Rafter O brand, boots, and starched jeans. The perfect picture of a ranching cowgirl. Janie was jealous. Not because Angie had always been the beautiful sister, but because she knew exactly who she was and her place in the world.

"Are you okay? Your lips are puffy and your face is red." Angie leaned closer and stared. "What happened?"

"Nothing. Let's just go."

Out of the corner of her eye, Janie noticed the deputy's vehicle turning the corner and heading their way. She tried to slink down in the seat and disappear, but it was no use. He honked and waved. She lifted a hand in response but did not turn her head to look at him.

"What was that about?" asked Angie as she backed into the street.

Might as well give her sister something to distract her from the kissing incident that Janie would never tell anyone about. Ever.

"He asked me out."

"Deputy Skinner?"

"Yes."

"When?"

"Saturday."

"Where ya going?"

"A movie."

"You said yes?"

"Yep."

"What about the fire chief?"

"What about him?"

Janie knew how to string her sister along and keep her off guard by giving her just enough information to warrant more questions, and never give her anything extra, which only created assumptions. From that it always turned into an entire discussion of what Janie should or should not do, what she most likely needed to do in the future, and a breakdown of the motivation behind her behavior. It really was exhausting.

"Something else happened," Angie observed.

"No, it didn't."

"You're acting weird."

"No, I'm not."

"Your cheeks are still flushed."

"Worked up a sweat sweeping out the shop."

"What else did you do today?"

"Nothing."

Janie could feel Angie studying her, but she didn't press the issue. Thank goodness they were pulling to a stop in front of Chimmi's shop. Janie couldn't get out of the truck fast enough to escape her sister's inquisition.

"Janie's got a date with Deputy Skinner," Angie announced as she entered the beauty shop. The resounding response erupted with whistles and catcalls. Janie tried to force a half-smile to her lips, but inside, she cringed. This would keep them entertained for the next hour, if only Janie could keep her mouth shut about the one thing that haunted her. She knew for a fact, it would be a long time before the memory of that kiss stopped stinging her lips.

Miss Hattie, with the stuck cat, sat under the dryer, her nose in a magazine. She glanced at Janie and nodded with a half-smile on her face.

"What's your pleasure?"

"Excuse me?" Janie looked at Karmelle, uncertain how to answer.

"What nail color do you want?"

"She wants fluorescent pink," Angie said as she sat in the pedicure chair and eased her feet into the warm, sudsy water.

Janie shook her head. "No. Any color but pink." She'd be laughed out of the county barn if any of the employees saw her working on a motor with hot pink fingernails.

Karmelle winked and led her to the back of the room where she settled into a chair at the nail station. "No worries. You'll love it when I'm done."

One corner at the back of the salon was sectioned off with wood flooring where a sleek, black lacquer manicure table stood. The wall was covered in shelving that held bottles of nail polishes in every color you could imagine with a hand-painted sign that read *Finger Paints*. Janie settled into a zebra-striped chair that was surprisingly comfy. Karmelle took her hands and placed them on a black and white foam pillow.

"Really, I don't want pink." Janie was a bit nervous since she had never had a manicure in her life. Her nervousness made her feel even sillier for agreeing to put herself at the mercy of these women.

"What are you wearing on your date?" Karmelle asked.

"I have no idea. Whatever I can pull out of the closet tomorrow night."

"That's my sister," Angie commented. "She's not one to plan or primp for a man."

"I'm really rough on my nails," Janie added. "I work at the county's mechanic shop."

"Yes, we know. This type of polish is very durable. You'd be surprised. An activator causes a chemical reaction which makes it adhere, and it will last at least two weeks."

Janie was skeptical. After it was finished, she'd find a way to remove it after she got home anyway. Money wasted. Maybe Angie would offer to pay since this was her idea anyway.

"So, tell me about this guy you're dating."

"She's going out with Deputy Skinner." Again, her sister. This hour was going to be excruciating.

"Don't know a thing about him," said Karmelle. "I haven't lived here very long."

Chimmi squealed, "He is a cutie! Very nice young man. Brave too."

"Did he grow up here?" Karmelle asked.

"Yes," Angie said, "went to high school the same time we did. At least two classes above you. Right, Janie?"

"Ooh, a high school romance," Karmelle teased.

"Actually, it was his little brother who she asked to the prom, but he turned her down." Angie said as she placed her feet on a towel.

Janie gritted her teeth and didn't offer any more information. Thanks to her sister, she couldn't keep any secrets apparently. She watched Karmelle file and buff her scraggly nails. Seemed silly wasting good polish on her hands.

"He saved the grocery store from being robbed, you know."

"Do tell." Karmelle stopped filing to turn her attention to Chimmi.

"I remember the day the grocery store was robbed," Miss Hattie yelled from under the dryer. "That Skinner boy saved the clerk. He's a county deputy now."

"How can she hear us from under the dryer?" Karmelle whispered.

Chimmi shrugged her shoulders. "As I was saying, it was a young couple who wandered around the store for some time until they finally decided on a can of beans and a box of crackers."

"No, it was a loaf of bread," squawked Miss Hattie.

"Okay, whatever. Anyway, Deputy Jack Skinner happened to be heading home after his shift and came in to buy a can of soda and find something for his supper. He usually eats every night at the diner, being a bachelor and all, but that night he just wanted to get home."

This time Miss Hattie raised the dryer and patted her rollers with the palms of her hand. "It had been a busy day. He was ready to get home."

"Yes, I already said that." Chimmi was losing her patience by the sound of her voice.

Janie was anxious for someone to get to the end of the story. It really was agonizing to listen while they argued over the details. She wondered how different the story would be when the deputy told it.

"For whatever reason, this couple—"

"They were possessed!" Miss Hattie made the point with much gusto by pointing a finger heavenward.

"The young woman pulled out a gun and pointed it at the clerk. The man told him to open the cash drawer or else. The clerk was so scared, he froze."

"That was Hulan and Margie's boy," Miss Hattie offered.

"At that precise second, Deputy Jack told them to cease and desist, the store clerk ducked behind the counter, the young man spun around, and the deputy beaned him right in the forehead with a Dr. Pepper."

"I heard it was Diet Coke." Angie joined in the conversation.

Janie audibly moaned and rolled her eyes heavenward. At this point, the three of them continued to argue over the details.

Karmelle giggled. "Sounds to me like you've got a date with the local hero."

She finished the filing and applied the first coat. Janie barely noticed the color. She may be going out with a remarkable lawman, but the only thing that kept crossing Janie's mind was the one thing she had promised herself never to think about ever again.

That kiss, which was fairly remarkable itself.

27

CHIMMI

AFTER JANIE AND ANGIE LEFT, THE GIRLS WERE assembled in the beauty shop, discussing the turn of events. They were waiting on Belinda, who was on her way to get caught up on the details.

"Can you think of any reason to cut Jack and Janie's date short on Saturday night?" Chimmi asked. She always assumed leadership at these brainstorming sessions. She knew the others would be on board and put any plan in motion once they decided on the right course of action.

Miss Hattie stuck her head out from under the dryer. "Maybe somebody can call in an emergency so the deputy has to come back to Dixon?"

The drink of choice was a delightful sweet peach, minty tea that Karmelle had created. Smiles appeared on every face, with a few sighs of delight when they saw Belinda through the picture window. She parked her car and emerged, balancing a white bakery box in one hand and her purse in the other. She pushed open the door with her behind.

"She showed up at the Henderson fire first. Beat the entire fire department there," Belinda said as she swept into the room. Chimmi took the box of treats, and Karmelle poured another glass of tea.

"We know. Here's your tea. Let me know how you like it."

Chimmi took a sip of tea and then took another before talking. "And she has a date with Skinner on Saturday."

"That needs to be broken up and quick. Jack is not the man for our Janie," said Belinda. They all nodded their heads in agreement.

Karmelle slipped into a salon chair, a look of concentration shadowing her face. "So, we have to bust up the date with the deputy and get Janie to spend some quality time with the fire chief. The only problem I see is that our victim is intensely unmanageable."

That brought laughter from the group.

"That's not a deterrent. We've been up against worse," Belinda pointed out as she handed out muffins. "Pumpkin and spice. It's a new concoction of mine."

Silence descended over the salon as the matchmakers concentrated on their muffins, until the door opened with a pronounced squeak and shut with a thud.

"Christy!" Chimmi said, as they all exchanged conspiratorial glances. "What can we help you with?"

"I need to make a hair appointment." Christy from the chamber stopped in front of the mirror and, with a heavy sigh, studied her reflection. "I need something lighter and brighter. And can you layer it around my face?"

"Sure. What's the special occasion?" Chimmi switched to her professional persona.

"Nothing. I just need a change."

"How's the fire chief?" Miss Hattie was never one to waste time on small talk.

Chimmi shot a cautious glance towards Christy, but there was no reason to be concerned. They weren't guilty of anything. Yet.

"He's been really busy lately. But he's just fine, thank you."

Knowing glances were exchanged.

"I know it's late, but if you have time now, I can work you in." Chimmi made a sweeping motion towards the salon chair she vacated. "Karmelle, pour Christy a glass of tea, would you please?"

"That's great," Christy said with a surprised look. "I really appreciate it."

"How are the Founders' Day plans coming?"

"It's really coming together nicely, I think," said Christy as she sat. "We've had a good response for parade entries, and several vendors from neighboring towns will be set up at the fairgrounds. I'm trying to talk the Lions Club into cooking pancakes that morning."

Chimmi dug through the antique armoire that served as her hair color supply cabinet. "You said lighter? This should work." She held up a tube of *Sunny Daze* color and squeezed it into a bowl to mix with another chemical.

Miss Hattie interrupted the conversation to relay her remembrances of the good ole' days in Dixon and the trouble she and her cousins used to cause. "The town square was the center of activity in those days, although it's not really a square, like most towns have. Every Saturday, we'd come to town. There was a band, kids setting up horse races, I got my first kiss behind the soda shop on Main." She giggled.

If you could call the intersection of Main Street and Main Avenue a town square. Dixon was not the county seat and did not have a courthouse, but it was the oldest town site in the county.

"I would have loved to have seen Dixon then," Christy bubbled.

They were enthralled with Miss Hattie's stories, although Chimmi wondered how much was actually true. Miss Hattie loved having a captive audience.

Chimmi suddenly had an idea. "What are you doing this Saturday?"

"Nothing that I know of."

"You should talk to Deputy Skinner. He's going to the movies in Amarillo."

"He is?"

"Heard he was taking Janie Olsen," Belinda offered.

"You should call Jack and then call Mack. Y'all could double date," Karmelle said as she filed a nail.

Chimmi stifled a grin while she tried to act completely oblivious to the conversation. She focused on wrapping pieces of foil around the colored strands on Christy's head instead of glancing at her sister. This could work. If they could get both couples in the same place, they could figure out a way to get two of them away, leaving Janie and Mack together.

The next hour was spent in pleasant conversation as Christy brought them up to speed on the events being planned by the Founders' Day Committee. Not only was Christy a good leader, but she was a good listener too. Of course, the girls at the salon had some ideas for her to consider.

"The committee meets again on Saturday afternoon. I will certainly pass along your input," Christy said as Chimmi spun her chair around to face the mirror. "I love it!"

The highlights did look good, although Christy was a

beautiful girl either way. The trim accentuated her eyes, and the sides fell just below her jaw line and tapered to a longer length in the back. It was almost the exact same cut she had given Janie, but Chimmi dared not mention that.

Belinda stood, a serious look of concentration on her face. "What about if my coffee shop provides refreshments for your committee meeting?"

"Thank you. That would be so nice of you. I know the committee would really appreciate it."

"It's all set then. Don't worry about it, I will bring something fabulously delicious, and I can bring something to drink too."

Christy paid Chimmi and then turned to give Belinda a hug. "That is so thoughtful of you. I will see you girls around. Thanks again, Chimmi. I love my hair."

She waved from the sidewalk outside before getting into her car.

"What was that all about?" Chimmi planted herself in front of Belinda. "Spill."

"I think I know of a way to cut the double date short. Say a prayer that it works and that true love prevails." Belinda grinned, her eyes sparkling with mischief.

"Whatever it is, count me in," said Chimmi.

"Oh, you're in, all right. You're all in because it's going to take every single one of us to pull this off without a hitch."

"I'll pour us another glass of tea," offered Karmelle.

28

JANIE

Saturday could not have come any sooner, and Janie was ready for a night out, even if it was with Deputy Skinner. They just didn't have anything in common, and Janie was horrible at small talk. At least part of the evening would be at a movie, which makes it impossible to talk. She hoped he wouldn't put his arm around her in the dark theater, the way guys usually did. Or, kiss her! Snap out of it, she told herself. She was an adult woman, for gosh sakes. A military vet.

She stood in front of her closet staring. Then held out her hands, fingers pointed like the model she wasn't. She would never admit it to her sister, but she really liked her nails. Not pink and not red, but a shade in between. Not too bright, but more subtle. She felt so girly, and that felt strange. Maybe she should wear a dress tonight, but she had no idea what shoes. What about her western boots again? They had looked all right at the livestock show.

In the back of her closet were a few dresses jammed together—a black one for funerals, a white cotton one for church, and a flowered one, midi length, her mother had brought home before Janie went into the Army. She held the trio up to her body and judged each in the mirror. After that spectacle, she resolved that she just couldn't do it. Maybe someday, but not this day. No dress. No way. Instead, she put on a pair of tight jeans, dark blue with a bit of bling on the back pockets. Maybe they were Angie's. She tucked the jean legs into her knee-high cowgirl boots. A light blue sweater that might've been an Angie hand-me-down completed the outfit. Turning this way and that, she scoped out her figure in the mirror. Looking good—pink nails and all.

"Let me do your makeup." Her younger sister Angie burst into the room. "I can't believe you actually said yes to a date."

Janie laughed. "I'm getting a little stir crazy, I think. Since I got back home from the military, the slower pace seems strange. And I don't need help. Thank you anyway."

"Okay, just some mascara. That's all I'm saying. I'll compromise and leave you alone."

Janie sighed. She dug into a dresser drawer.

"Don't you dare!" Angie snatched the tube from Janie's hand. "That's got to be fifteen years old or more. You'll get an eye infection."

"You're being a bit dramatic, don't you think?"

"Do you want to go blind?" Angie looked at her like she was dumb as a rock. "I think there's an unopened tube in the bathroom."

"How old is that one?"

"It's fairly new. I keep a spare."

Janie paused to look at her sister. "Why are you here and not at your house? And come to think of it, why aren't you going out on a date?"

Angie's eyes turned sad and then she jutted out her

chin. "I have successfully run off the only guy who really cared for me. It's hard to undo that kind of mistake."

"Well, I've never even found a man who truly cares for me. I don't think he exists."

Angie collapsed on the bed, lying on her back and staring at the ceiling. "We are quite the pair. True love is so elusive. I just want to work cows and ride as many miles across the Rafter O Ranch as possible in my lifetime."

"At least you have a plan." Janie closed one eye and carefully took a swipe, getting a blob of black on her cheek.

"Let me do it." Angie expertly blackened her eyelashes. "Close your eyes."

She applied eye color and lip gloss.

"That's enough." Janie stopped her.

"You really are beautiful, Janie. You have a glow that you didn't have before. I think it's a newfound confidence."

"But being back here in this room makes me remember that I'll always be just Plain Jane."

"Oh, dear sister, you're far from plain. Those guys from high school are eating their hearts out now, like one of them whose name is Jack Skinner."

Janie stood and kissed the top of Angie's head. "You're just saying that because you're my sister, and I love you for it. Thanks."

Her mother called up the stairs, "Janie, Deputy Jack is here."

Embarrassment tingled through her body. Her mother was actually calling for her from downstairs? Could this night start out any worse? She grabbed a tiny crossbody purse just to hold her license, money, and a lip gloss.

"Hey, that's my purse and lip gloss." Angie squinted.

Janie grinned. "Thanks, dear sister. I owe you."

Angie followed Janie down the stairs. Never ladylike the way her sisters were, her mother always said she sounded like a herd of elephants when she ran through the house as a kid. "You're my tomboy," her mom had called her.

Deputy Jack smiled at her appearance. "You look great, Janie. Hey, Angie." Then he said his polite good-byes to Mrs. Olsen, who stood in the entry hall beaming at the three of them. Angie followed the couple outside.

Stepping aside, Jack allowed Janie to lead the way to his truck and then he hurried around her to open the passenger door.

"Try to have some fun, you two," Angie called out.

"Well, you would certainly know about that," Janie replied. They all shared a laugh. Janie gave her sister a quick wave as they drove away.

As Deputy Jack Skinner turned onto the caliche road, he glanced over at Janie, who fidgeted with her seatbelt and hair and folded her hands to hide her nails.

"You look real nice tonight, Janie."

She wiped the hair from her forehead. "Uh, thanks. Hey, is the A/C on? Feels a little warm in here to me."

"It's not exactly hot outside. Do you really need the air?"

She let out a breath. "No, it's okay. If you're comfortable, so am I."

"Well, just let me know. I aim to please, ma'am." Then he let out a kind of strange laugh. She whipped her head towards him and stared. Was it like a donkey? Or a hyena. She imagined living with someone her whole life who laughed like that. Nope, shoot me now.

"I have a huge favor to ask." He hesitated. Janie turned to look at him with interest.

"What is that?"

"I need you to do some work on my cop car, if you have time." Jack said as Janie settled into the leather seats. He did look handsome in a uniform, and in regular clothes too, which he wore for their date.

"Sure. Not much going on at the shop next week, that I know of. What are we doing to it?"

"I need to go at least two hundred."

Janie turned to look at him in surprise. "Two hundred miles per hour? Are you crazy?"

"That's what I need. We have a couple of brothers with a souped-up Charger and I'm going to catch them. I'm tired of eating their dust."

She noticed the muscles in his jaw clench and the determined jut of his chin. "How are they breaking the law?"

"Excessive speed through the city limits, vandalism, trespassing, and we have an increase in rural burglaries. We think it's them."

Janie creased her forehead. "I might be able to do it, but we have to lighten the frame in some way. Would you say your vehicle has good aerodynamics? Of course, I won't know for sure until I get under the hood."

"I would really appreciate it if you could take a look. We've never had a real mechanic before. I think Big Jim learned everything he knows from his daddy, who worked for the county before him."

"I learned everything I know from watching my grandfather work on tractors, and then the military was a good training ground. I got to experience every kind of engine and vehicle you can imagine, and then some. I really enjoyed my job."

"So why are you back in Dixon?"

She paused. How many times had she pondered that question in her own mind? Countless. Mainly because she had no easy answer, and she had no life. Janie could not think of one good reason to come back to the ranch, other than she had nowhere else to go.

Jack cleared his throat. "Sounds like the Founders' Day celebration is coming together. Your family must be excited."

"Actually, we have been so busy my parents haven't even mentioned it, but yes, it is a wonderful tribute to my ancestors who decided on settling in this county. After he obtained the land, he set up a trading post in his dugout. And then he established a town plat and applied with the state. Many of the Olsens followed him to Texas after that. A great uncle had the first post office in his house, and his wife, Aunt Maybelline, was the first teacher."

"Wow, what a legacy."

"It should be a fun day. It really is nice of the chamber to recognize us."

"If you would allow me, I would be happy to escort you to the banquet."

"Thanks, Jack." She looked at him in surprise, but she was a bit suspicious. She had never had any man pay this much attention to her and actually be interested in anything that she might be involved in. Angie's voice echoed in her ear. *Have fun.*

29

JANIE

THE DRIVE TO THE BIG CITY CONTINUED IN silence, enough so that it became awkward and uncomfortable, to say the least. The only thing they found in common to talk about were the kids they went to high school with. Where they were now, who still lived in Dixon, and who had moved away. Of course, as a county deputy, he knew everyone. Janie couldn't really remember anyone, and she was embarrassed to admit it, but she had no interest in knowing where any of her classmates were. Once she had moved away, she left that part of her life behind. She had no intention of ever returning, yet here she was.

"This is the place." Jack parked on a side street in downtown Amarillo. "It's a short walk. I forgot to ask, how does Mexican food sound?"

"That sounds perfect."

The light was fading behind the high-rise buildings and dusk descended on the busy streets. They stepped off the street into vintage old-world Mexico. Stucco walls and twinkling lights were the backdrop for handcrafted furniture. The atmosphere was relaxing and the smells of grilling meat made her smile. As they walked in, he casually rested an arm on her shoulders. She didn't shrug it off, but she wasn't sure how she felt about it either.

The hostess seated them on a covered patio, complete with a trickling fountain, leafy green plants, and vibrant Saltillo tile. Janie settled in behind an oversized menu. Maybe a platter with one of everything? She was famished.

"Surprise! I'm so happy we found y'all!"

A screech and a giggle sliced through the peaceful mood and etched a chill up the middle of Janie's spine. She peeped over her menu to see Christy from the chamber, that's how she knew her because she had no idea what her last name might be. Her stomach flip-flopped, and not from hunger, as she looked at Mack, his dark eyes like a laser beam hitting hers. For once he wasn't wearing a firefighter's cap or helmet. His dark hair was a little long on top, but neatly trimmed on the sides and back, almost military-issue. Her heart thudded, at the same time, a cloud of dread descended over her mood.

"Hey, Jack." The blonde leaned down with an air kiss in the direction of his cheek and stood to flick her wrist with a wave at Janie. "Julie, right?"

"Janie, actually."

"Well, *Jane*, don't you look cute." Christy glanced at Janie's legs under the table. "I used to wear my jeans and boots like that some years ago, but now I have to dress more professionally. You know, chamber president and all that." Her bubbly giggle was piercing.

Janie looked the other girl up and down, from her low neckline revealing her buxom stature, down to the hem of her tailored dress and stylish heels. She certainly fit the part she played, and she was a beautiful girl. Janie felt even more self-conscious, underdressed, and wished she hadn't worn jeans, but then again, it didn't matter what she wore. No one would notice her anyway.

Jack stood. The men shook hands, and Jack leaned close to give Christy a hug. "Did you do something different with your hair?"

"Yes, actually I did, and thanks for noticing, Jack."

Mack placed his hand on Christy's lower back as he used the other hand to pull out and move up her chair.

"When I saw Jack the other day, he mentioned y'all might be here, so I roped Mack into taking me into the city too. We haven't been on a double date in ages."

Mack forced a half-smile as he took his seat. The waitress suddenly appeared with additional silverware and two more big menus. Janie disappeared once again behind hers without offering hellos. Chicken, but she didn't trust herself to speak. Why did he have to be here?

She had decided to take her sister's advice for once, and just enjoy herself. No pressure to make an impression. Easier said than done with Mack sitting across the table from her. She pressed her lip-glossed mouth together and blinked her mascara-tipped lashes. Was she pretending to be something she wasn't? She should have just stayed home.

Janie finally had to lower the menu so that the waitress could hear her order, and they all sat in an awkward silence. Conversation was minimal as they waited for their food. Janie concentrated on not looking at Mack, although her mouth still tingled from the memory of his kiss as though his lips had burned her. *Don't look at him. Do not look.*

"Janie."

She started and glanced at Jack.

"Do you want a refill on your tea?"

She had been focusing on not looking at Mack and hadn't noticed the waitress standing next to her with a tea pitcher.

Once everyone relaxed a bit more, the fire chief and the deputy talked city business while Christy chimed in her two cents every so often. Janie was content to sit in silent oblivion with no one paying her any mind.

The men began to exchange stories while Christy and Janie laughed. And Janie cringed every time Deputy Jack snorted with that hyena gurgle, but Mack was a funny storyteller.

When their food was delivered, Christy picked at her sparse salad. Janie dug into her beef enchilada platter, while both men had beef fajitas.

"You must exercise a lot." Christy raised her eyebrows as Janie wolfed down her food. "I can't eat that stuff anymore, or it'll pack the pounds on me. Plus, they say red meat is not the healthiest for people to eat. Plant-based, that's the way to go nowadays."

Janie almost stared daggers at Christy. Then directed some towards Mack.

"I run," was all she said at first. Then added, "Plus, we are a state of beef producers. I think the Rafter O turns out some of the healthiest protein on the planet."

"That's right," Deputy Jack interjected, "we are in Texas, Christy, known as the beef capital of the world. Better not say that too loudly about it not being healthy. Might start a shootout." Then he laughed his hyena laugh. This time Janie appreciated it.

Christy stroked Mack's bicep and looked starry-eyed. "My sweety understands me. I try to stay current with the latest trends and read up on all the research." Looking at Janie, she said, "One must exercise one's mind as well as her body, you know." A fake smile sat on her face.

One must shut up, and one must stop looking at me. Janie cleared her throat.

Mack used his napkin, then said, "Janie was in the military. I'm sure they trained her to use her brain as well as her body."

Janie stared at him. Was he defending her? And why had the conversation suddenly turned to the topic of her? She decided not to comment.

"What was that like? Being with all those men. Where did you undress? And shower?" Christy fanned her face and giggled. "I've always wondered about that."

Janie wondered about men who liked girls like this one. Why was Mack dating her anyway?

"There were a couple of showers designated for the women. And sometimes, in the barracks, we all changed clothes together. We became a team and didn't look at each other as male and female."

"Oh, I cannot believe that. Seriously? Men are men, and if there is a woman in the same room taking her clothes off, I am sure a man is going to sneak a peek." Christy bubbled over with laughter. Then with a straight face and a low whisper, she asked, "Did any of them ever come on to you? You know what I mean. Make a pass."

Janie looked at Mack, but answered Christy. "There was only one time. I kneed the guy in the crotch and flipped him to the ground. Word got around to never mess with me."

"Oh, my, really? You're kind of macho aren't you, *Jane?*" She grabbed Mack's arm and leaned her head against his shoulder. "Me. I like being girly and having a big strong man to protect me. Right, honeybun?"

Mack grunted and kept eating. But also raised his eyes to look at Janie.

Deputy Jack put an arm around Janie's shoulders. "Well, thanks for warning me, soldier. I will mind my manners for sure." Again, that hyena laugh that sent a chill up Janie's spine and shot through her brain like a dagger.

Janie kept her cool and tried not to let Christy's ridiculous comments get to her. The rest of the evening was spent in easy conversation with Christy filling them in on the upcoming Founders' Day celebration. Janie listened with interest, and she had to admit the girl earned her keep and had a talent for organizing events. The day was going to be a nice tribute to her family.

"Oh, and the best part is we have ordered a plaque that will be placed at the corner of Main Street and Main Avenue in honor of the Olsens, the town's founding family. We'll have the unveiling sometime that day." She beamed. "I'm still working on the details."

While the others continued to eat, Christy kept talking.

"We had a committee meeting this afternoon. It's going to be epic!" She talked with her hands, excitement shining in her eyes. "There's a parade. Mack, you missed the meeting, but we need you to organize the entries. I want to lead with the fire engine."

Jack leaned forward with interest. Mack frowned.

"And we added a 5K race. Costs twenty dollars to enter. But you get a T-shirt! I designed it myself and ordered them today." Christy was bubbling again. "All proceeds will go to charity—probably the fire department."

Deputy Jack turned to Janie. "You should enter. You're a runner, aren't you?"

She nodded, and Mack looked at her.

Christy jumped in. "Well, I won't be entering the race. I'll have my hands full coordinating the whole day. I didn't realize what a big job it would be. But you know me, I am up for the challenge." She displayed a big toothy smile for her tablemates, and even looked around the restaurant at other diners, as though she were collecting votes for political office.

The men paid the check and Janie smiled, partly to be friendly and partly with relief that they were about to part ways. The more she hung around the fire chief, the more he stayed in her mind. And he was beginning to affect her heart too, and that was most certainly a hopeless cause. Out of sight, out of mind was the only way to roll in this situation.

They stood up from the table and walked to the front entrance, Jack placing his hand in the small of her back. She tried not to cringe outwardly, but inwardly, she was uncomfortable. She was not ready for this relationship to go anywhere. She stepped outside to see Mack watching them intently.

As they exited into the night, the air was damp with the chill of an early spring. She took a deep breath. The night was perfect, but she had the wrong man on her arm.

"Where're we going next?" Christy asked.

30

MACK

As the two couples stood on the street corner in downtown Amarillo, all heads turned to Christy as she suddenly took off down the sidewalk.

"There's a coffee shop just around the corner on Polk Street," she said over her shoulder. The others fell in line behind her without argument.

Mack liked the cozy feel of wood, combined with the sleek, corrugated tin walls, decorated with black and white photographs. Even though he had just eaten every bite of the fajitas, the aroma of roasting coffee beans made him crave a cup. They all settled into a corner booth and placed their orders.

Mack concentrated on his Americano and tried not to look at Janie, but he could not get that kiss out of his head. Sure, Christy was as shiny as a new penny. And familiar.

Janie was solid. Strong-willed. Her silence only enhanced the intelligence that burned in her eyes. She was so near. He wished he could touch her. The reality of not being able to only made his stomach tie up in knots. This double date had been a terrible idea.

"Weren't you the first one at the fire on Henderson's farm?" Christy turned the conversation to Janie. All heads turned her way.

"Yes, I was."

"We discussed the entire incident at the firehouse meeting on Thursday," Deputy Jack said.

Mack cleared his throat. He noticed the high flush that covered Janie's cheeks at the mention of the fire-house. Thursday. She remembered that kiss, too.

Christy's purse buzzed. "Excuse me. I should get this. It might be a committee member." She tapped the screen and then shouted. "Oh, no!"

They all looked at her with curiosity. Mack felt certain it was nothing of much importance. Christy's crises were usually self-induced because not much ever happened in Dixon to create a Chamber of Commerce emergency.

"The chamber office got broken into. They want me to come back right away."

"That's not good." Jack assumed his serious deputy face and sat up straighter in his chair. "Did they break a window? What's missing?"

"I'm not sure. The mayor wants me to look over everything."

"I can take you back." Jack then turned to Janie. "I'm sorry to cut our date short, but there may be a burglar loose in the county."

"I completely understand. You go do your job."

"I'll give Janie a ride home," offered Mack. He hoped his voice sounded calm and nonchalant, but his heart pounded inside his chest. Another chance to be alone with Janie scared him to death.

Christy stood and gave Mack a peck on the cheek.

"I'll call you as soon as I know what happened. Good-night, *Jane*. Sorry to steal your date."

Janie shrugged and gave her a wave. Jack leaned down to kiss her cheek, but she dodged it, which turned into an awkward half-hug, half-body bump.

"Maybe we can try this again next week?" he asked.

Janie didn't respond, just nodded her head. Mack wasn't sure what that meant. He always had a hard time reading women.

Mack and Janie sat in silence after the other two left. She seemed to be enjoying her coffee, and he hated to ruin the moment. He liked the silence as well and was comfortable. Her presence made him calmer, relaxed. He had noticed before, she had that effect on people.

"Stop staring at me."

"I didn't know I was." He cleared his throat and fidgeted in his chair. "Sorry." He raked his fingers through his hair. "About what happened at the meeting." He paused, not sure what to say next.

"It didn't happen. Don't ever bring it up again." She sipped her coffee, avoiding his eyes.

He swallowed the lump in his throat. "Let's get out of here, if you're finished with your coffee." He stood and held out his hand.

She turned wary eyes in his direction, took another sip of coffee, and then shrugged her shoulders. "Why, not." She placed her hand in his and followed him to the door.

They walked in silence towards his pickup, his confidence failing when she pulled her hand from his. He held the pickup truck door open for her and when he had buckled in and turned the ignition, she finally asked, "Where are we going?"

"To an event I've been wanting to attend ever since I

heard about it. I'm thinking you might like it too, after you get over the initial shock."

"Okay. Are you going to give me any hints?"

"No. This will be a total surprise. A spontaneous adventure. I think you can handle it though." He smiled at her.

"You're just teasing me now. I can't think of anything relating to an adventure that could possibly happen in Amarillo, Texas."

He laughed, always surprised at her wit and quick comebacks. "Well, you just might be in for the shock of your life."

She didn't try to question him further but sat patiently in silence as he turned west on Sixth Street. After leaving the downtown area, he noticed more and more cars were parked on either side of the street, and then he heard the music.

"We may have to walk a ways," he said as he parallel parked on a side street several blocks off Sixth.

Curiosity formed on her face, but Janie did not ask any more questions. He grinned at her as they met at the back of the pickup truck. He took her hand again and they walked towards the sounds of a screaming steel guitar.

She smiled. "A biker rally! You're taking me to a biker rally?"

The smile was enough for him. He could go home a contented man after seeing the excitement on Janie's face.

"A Harley-Davidson rally, to be more exact."

This time she didn't pull her hand away, and they merged into the crowd. Harleys were angled along both sides of the street in one section, while food vendors filled up another. Mack stopped to buy a bag of pork rinds, freshly fried, and dusted with cinnamon and sugar.

"Oh, I don't think I could eat another bite after that dinner we had," she said, but then reached into the bag and put a piece in her mouth. "Wow. These are good."

He grabbed her hand again and tugged her closer to the stage. They were surrounded by people in leathers and bandanas tied over their heads or around their necks. The crowd swayed with the music, seemingly unaware of the level of noise. Mack polished off the bag of pork rinds and tossed the bag in a trash can, but before he could ask if she wanted anything to drink, the band slowed the tempo considerably. "Want to dance?"

"I guess," was her reply.

She followed him to the center of the parking lot that had been blocked off for a dance floor. Although he was almost a foot taller than Janie, they seemed to fit together perfectly. He pulled her close, her head at his chest, so she laid a cheek against him. The scent of her nearness consumed him. He couldn't think. He couldn't see anything. He could only think of the warmth of her body against his.

The song ended way too soon and they stood there for a split second in each other's arms before Janie pulled away.

"I'm ready to go home," she said, with no further explanation.

Before he could ask her what was wrong, a scraggly man stepped in between them. "Why so glum, little lady? You need one of these." He proceeded to tie a bright purple do-rag on top of her head. She laughed.

"It says CHILL on the side here. Looks good on you." Mack put an arm around her shoulder and leaned close to whisper in her ear. "Please, stay."

She led him away from the crowd and down a few blocks, where she found an empty bench under an elm tree decorated with twinkling lights.

"Why did you bring me here?"

He had a hard time finding any words. She looked beautiful with that purple do-rag, her hair laying on either side of her face, and her cheeks flushed from their hurried walk. A thousand different answers ran through his head, but he realized that Janie was different. She wouldn't settle for anything less than the truth. No games. No pretense.

"I used to come to these rallies before I dated Christy. I wanted to bring her last year, but she doesn't like things like this. She's more into dressing up and eating at fancy places. I just thought you might like it, that's all."

"Oh, I get it. I'm not fancy enough for some places like she is, but you can drag me to a street dance. No problem."

"What are you talking about? It's not an insult that I brought you here." He watched her fume for a minute and stare at him through squinted eyes. Then she laughed.

"You're right. I do like stuff like this. Let's go look at some bikes." This time she was the one who held out a hand, so he took it.

She suddenly spun on one heel and faced him, pointing a finger in his face. "No kissing."

He turned loose and held up both hands in defeat. "I promise... maybe."

"Wipe that grin from your face. I mean it. I have been a Harley fan for a long time, and I don't need any distractions. I really do want to look at the bikes."

"Okay. I will be on my best behavior, ma'am."

They walked back into the crowd, wandering around the parked bikes and meeting the owners. His heart swelled every time she asked an intelligent question to one of the bikers. She wanted to know every detail, and they were thrilled to share. Mack had never known a woman who knew as much about Harleys as he did. And he tried to keep his promise, but every time she stood back to admire the details of a bike and then spouted off the year and model, he wanted to swing her around and kiss her face off.

They walked the street, danced some more, drank ice-cold lemonade around midnight, and then the town began to roll up the streets and they had to head back towards his pickup.

"That was nice," Janie said, their fingers still laced together. He unlocked the vehicle and held the door open for her. She stifled a yawn with her hand.

"This can't go anywhere." She stared at him, the dome light illuminating her face.

"Why not?"

"You have a girlfriend, and I'm leaving soon. Besides, I'm not your type."

"What is my type?" He started the engine and drove through the dark neighborhood, weaving his way towards the interstate.

"Christy's your type."

"It wasn't until tonight that I realized that Christy and I have absolutely nothing in common. Besides, you need to stay in Dixon and fill in for Big Jim, save your money so you can buy your own Harley."

He waited for an answer, but none came. When he glanced over, Janie had rested her head against the window and was sound asleep.

"You are absolutely my type," he whispered.

31

CHIMMI

THE CURL UP & DYE SHOP WAS BUZZING WITH customers, all the regulars were getting something done. One sat under the dryer and another had her feet soaking. Chimmi had just finished giving a cut and Karmelle was straightening her manicure table after Angie. Janie was next.

The main topic of conversation was the upcoming Founders' Day event, including the parade.

Angie was letting her nails dry and Janie was next in the chair, talking with Angie and Karmelle while she waited. "I could almost get used to this pampering. At least Karmelle is able to get all the grease out from under my nails. Even if it takes more than one soak."

The three shared a laugh.

"We'll be riding some of our horses in the parade," Angie told the customers. "Nathan, Travis, and I will bring a few of our best."

"I hear Leonard from the hardware store is driving his classic car, a T-bird, I think." Karmelle's eyelashes fluttered.

"Stop fluttering those eyelashes at the mention of his name." Chimmi pointed a finger at her sister.

"It's just a bit of dust," was Karmelle's quick answer.

Chimmi smiled. "We're taking a big ad out in the program. Full page. With a coupon, ladies. Be sure to clip it out. Twenty percent."

"Ooh, great. Can it be used for hair and nails?" one of the ladies asked.

Everyone was excited.

"Whatever your little heart desires." Chimmi looked up as the front door buzzed, and in walked Christy. She was wearing a straight skirt, heels, and a shimmering pink silk blouse.

"Hello ladies! How is everyone on this beautiful day?"

Not many answered, although they did give her polite smiles.

"Karmelle, do you think you could touch up my nails? Look at what happened?" Christy's bottom lip formed a pout.

She thrust her hand almost in front of Janie's face as Karmelle was painting her nails. Janie leaned her body off to one side and her brow furrowed.

"As you can see, I'm working on Janie right now. If you'd like to take a seat and wait, I think I can squeeze you in before my next one."

"Oh, Karmelle, I'm sure *Jane* wouldn't mind. I only have a couple to fix. You could do mine, lickity split, and then you can get right back to working on... the... uh... mechanic."

The salon's atmosphere changed to icy stillness as hair dryers were lifted to the off position and Chimmi's blow dryer was silenced.

"I only lack a few more minutes with Janie, and then

NATALIE BRIGHT & DENISE F. MCALLISTER

you're next, Christy. Tell us about the break-in while you wait."

With a deep frown, Christy perched on the edge of a zebra-striped chair, looking from one to the other, making sure she had everyone's attention. "It was the craziest thing. Someone had opened the women's restroom window and left it open. Walter noticed it on his rounds that evening. I had to dash right back from Amarillo."

"Was there anything missing?" Chimmi asked.

"Oh, papers were moved about and filing cabinet drawers were left open, but nothing was taken as far as I could tell."

"What a relief." Chimmi cleared her throat.

"Okay, now ladies, I'd like to address the elephant in the room. We all know this is a small town. And we love our small town. But, good Lord, we all know one another's business, don't we? For instance, I happen to know, because various people have reported this to me, that *Jane*, our county mechanic, took a little ride the other day on the back of *my* boyfriend's motorbike, with him driving it, of course. By the way, it was nearly sunset." Christy's head moved up and down like a bobblehead doll at a carnival.

Angie's eyes grew wide and she stared at Janie. Karmelle kept painting and Janie watched the work on her nails instead of making eye contact with anyone.

Christy stood and pivoted on her high heels as though she were on stage and continued her address to the women.

"Residents reported to me that they were seen... the perpetrators, I mean... at Main and Main, and *Jane* here had her arms wrapped tightly around my boyfriend's body. Someone else, who happened to be out cruising on the highway that evening, believes they could identify the two of them as headed towards Palo Duro Canyon, for who knows what reason." Christy shook her head, raised her hands, palms up, and then appeared to wipe her eyes.

Janie turned her head and started to speak, "Just a minute..."

But Christy cut her off. "Tsk, tsk, please don't interrupt me, *Jane*. I am almost finished. I just wanted to share with *my* friends here that when I first heard about this sce-nar-io, I felt a little sad, that maybe I was being deceived or that maybe this... uh... woman was after my boyfriend and had ill intentions. Truthfully, I think all my fretting caused me to snag my nails. But then I came to my senses. I realized that this is our county mechanic we're talking about. It's not like they were on a date. Perhaps Mack was having trouble with his motorbike, and they needed to take it for a spin so that *Jane* could then take a look at the mechanics of it. That's what she does, right? In fact, I'm not sure why she is getting her nails done. Won't they just get greasy again?"

Christy let out a half-mad, sickening giggle.

Chimmi stared at Karmelle and Janie, then at Christy. What in the world was going to come out of that girl's mouth next? Chimmi wondered if she should stop it before it went any further. She was the owner, after all. How should she word it to ask Christy to apologize?

Before Chimmi could think of what to say, Christy straightened her back, chest out, nose up, and looked around the room at all the women, her eyes welling up with tears. Her ever-present phony smile was affixed to her face.

Chimmi wondered if this was the moment that nail polish bottles were going to be thrown or hair was going to be pulled.

"Needless to say," Christy said calmly after taking a breath, "I spoke to Mack about this, and he assures me that *Jane* is a county employee and he would never compromise his employment, or mine, by carrying on with the mechanic. But then I was called away from a double-date to check on a break-in at the chamber office. Funny thing is, Mack failed to call me when he got home. From reliable sources, I've heard that he got home well after midnight."

She walked closer to Janie, stopping right behind Karmelle. "Jack and I came back here to go through my office. Where did you and Mack go from the time we left Amarillo until after midnight? Are you chasing after my boyfriend?"

Janie stood and pushed her chair back so fast it toppled over. She took a paper towel and tried to rub the polish off, doing a royal job of smearing it into a disastrous mess. She muttered, "Sorry" to Karmelle and then to Angie, "I'm outta here."

Christy continued to smile and spun around in the middle of the room. "Thank you, ladies, for listening to my sad little tale. And, Karmelle, do you think you could fix my nails? Appears you just got an opening."

Both Olsen sisters headed for the door, with Janie pulling on Angie, who looked as though she might deck Christy on her way out. The door swung shut behind them.

Chimmi stood. "Ladies, I'm sorry to say the shop is closed."

"But it's still early," one of them said.

Her face took on a calm appearance. But it was a deadly calm, like before a hurricane on the sea. And it was red.

"If you are in the middle of getting your hair done, you may stay. Everyone else, please leave. For circumstances beyond my control, I must close the shop now."

She stared directly at Christy and walked over to hold the front door open.

"What about my nails?" Christy whined.

Chimmi got within two inches of Christy's face. "The shop is closed."

Having no choice but to walk through the door, Christy huffed her exasperation as she went.

Chimmi slammed the door and flipped the sign to the "Closed" position.

She turned around to face the remaining patrons who had all broken out in smiles and loud applause.

"That could have gone better, but I suppose it went all right. That Christy is no pushover." Karmelle patted her sister. "I know you, so stop fuming about it. What's done is done."

"I never imagined Christy kept such close tabs on Mack. They always seem to go their separate ways most of the time. And why was the chamber office messy? That wasn't in our plan."

"It was me. While you kept a lookout and Belinda served muffins to the committee, I opened the restroom window and slipped into a back office to leave evidence."

"I wasn't the one keeping a lookout. That was supposed to be you." Chimmi placed her hands on her hips and gave Karmelle an exasperated stare. It wasn't the first time.

"It's done, but the main thing in all of this is our plan

worked. Mack and Janie obviously had a good time in each other's company."

"I guess you're right. We'll wait and see if our meddling did any good."

32

JANIE

"JUST GET ME OUT OF HERE!" JANIE PLEADED with Angie. "Take me back to work."

"Okay, okay. It'll be okay. Get in the truck," her sister said. "But we haven't eaten yet."

"This lunch break is over."

Christy came whirling past them, her high heels clicking on the cement walk.

Janie's head, and heart, were about to explode. She was mortified. Humiliated. Visions of high school when kids made fun of her filled her mind. When was she ever going to put that behind her?

She dropped her crossbody bag and the towel she had been using to rub the polish off onto the sidewalk. Stupid manicures. What business did she have being in that beauty shop anyway?

As she stumbled to collect everything and get to her feet, she ran smack dab into Deputy Jack, who was bent over trying to help her. "Hey, Janie. How are you doing?"

She stared, mouth open, like a terrified animal.

"You don't look so good. Are you all right?" He grabbed her arms.

"Fine. Let me go." She pulled away to head toward the truck.

"Janie," he called after her, "I just saw Mack down the street. Said he wanted to talk to you."

Fuming, maybe she should talk to Mack, give him a piece of her mind. The big jerk. Yeah, she was a county employee, the mechanic, and that's all she'd ever be in this town.

"Where is he?" she yelled at the deputy.

He paused, then answered, "I saw him at the florist. Looked like he was getting flowers for Christy." A partial smile was forming on his face, then he cut it short.

That just made her blood boil more. Flowers for Christy. Of course, he had to make nice with her after spending an evening with another woman. Why had she gone to that rally in the first place? She should have insisted he take her home right after dinner. As Janie climbed into Angie's truck, she was mumbling to herself, never saying goodbye to the deputy.

"Sure, make fun of me. Kiss me, then tell your girl-friend and everyone in town that I'm just the county mechanic, an employee." She didn't feel that insignifi-cant at the Harley rally. He danced with her. Held her hand.

Angie backed the truck out of the parking space and as they headed down Main, she looked over at her sister.

"What are you mumbling about, Janie? Are you all right? I know it was pretty crazy back there. That Christy sure is a piece of work."

"Do *not* say her name!" Janie's face looked deranged.

Angie kept driving and didn't say a word.

"There he is!" Janie pointed. "There he is! Pull over!"

"What are you going to do, Janie? Don't make a fool of yourself."

"I'm gonna tell him what a jerk he is. Pull over!"

Angie pulled over behind Mack's motorcycle as he walked from the florist, a giant bouquet of multicolored flowers in his hand.

When he noticed the truck and saw Janie marching towards him, he stopped and greeted her with a big smile, which suddenly turned to a look of concern when he saw her face.

"Janie. Something wrong?"

She tried to ignore how good he looked in his uniform, holding a full bouquet of flowers, walking closer to her with one arm extended like he was about to hug her. That only made her more furious. She was livid and launched into the tirade that had been brewing ever since Christy had uttered the first word of her dressing-down lecture in the beauty shop.

"Mr. Fire Chief. I'll tell you what's wrong. Sorry to interrupt your purchase of flowers for your sweetheart. Is this on company time, or is it your lunch hour? Maybe the mayor needs a report about your behavior, because apparently, you enjoy stringing two women along at the same time. Me, I'm really good about watching my time... punching my time card, since, after all, I'm just a county employee, the vehicle mechanic."

He looked at Angie, who shrugged slightly, then back at Janie.

"I have no idea what you're talking about, Janie. And if you must know, this *is* my lunch hour. And if you want to know who the flowers are for, you are more than welcome to follow me."

With that, he secured the flowers in one of his saddlebags, and adjusted his sunglasses and helmet. She stood blankly as he walked away and swung a leg over his fire engine red Harley.

"Janie, c'mon. Get in the truck. Let's go." Angie spoke calmly, obviously worried about her sister.

Before he started his bike, he turned to look at Angie. "Just follow me, okay?"

The low exhaust sound vibrated in her chest. She loved that sound and wanted more than anything to climb on behind him and forget about reality while the world whizzed by in a blur.

She didn't speak to her sister after getting back in the pickup truck. They drove a little while, and Janie was quiet, as if in a trance. She was replaying everything Christy had said in the beauty shop. And then a picture came to her mind of Mack holding those flowers, looking all handsome in his shades and uniform.

"Look, Janie, there he is. We're stopping."

As Angie pulled to a stop at the wrought iron fence, Janie watched Mack place the bouquet on the ground. They were close enough for Mack to hear the truck, and he turned to look. Their eyes met and locked.

Angie got out of the truck. "You coming?"

Reluctantly, Janie got out too and followed her through the arched gates.

The girls stood on either side of Mack. The red granite marker had GRIFFITT printed across the top.

"Today is my father's birthday." He kneeled and gently placed the flowers at the base of the headstone.

Janie backed away in horror. She had assumed and overreacted and made a fool of herself. What was it about that man that caused her to lose all control? Without another word, she hurried back to their vehicle. She watched Angie place a hand on Mack's shoulder and mutter a few words, and then she walked back to the truck.

"Oh my gosh, what have I done? Please take me back to work, Angie."

"What is going on with you two?" Angie asked.

Janie's throat closed as tears clouded her eyes. Maybe it was for the best. It's over, and it should have never started anyway. Typical of small towns, she was only adding to the fuel of the gossip mill. She just hoped Christy wouldn't sabotage the upcoming celebration and embarrass the Olsen family because of what she had done.

Grace had always told her children to pray and pray big. Turn your troubles over to God.

33

JANIE

After she had pulled on the work overalls, Janie plopped into the cracked vinyl chair and placed both boots on the desk. Guilt stained her like a greasy shop rag. She never meant to unleash such anger and hatred towards Mack. He had done nothing to her, and considering the situation, Christy had every right to be mad.

Yes, she had kissed another woman's boyfriend. But he kissed her first. And that night at the Harley rally would go on record as one of the best nights of her life. There had never been anyone before Mack who she felt so comfortable with, nor anyone she had had so much in common with. The reality was dire.

The truth of the matter was that she had it bad for the Dixon city fire chief. Coming back home had been a huge mistake, one that she would regret for the rest of her life, because it was going to take that long to forget him.

Her mother had always taught her to trust that God will fix the broken parts of your life. All you have to do is talk to Him. Janie felt ashamed to pray for the impossible. Mack would never be interested in a girl like her. A city fire chief had a reputation to uphold and needed someone at his side to reflect his importance in the community. The Plain Jane with grease under her fingernails was not the girl for him. Mack would always be the prettier one in their relationship. It was so sad and hopeless, it helped to make a joke. *I understand, God, and I'm okay with my life the way it is.*

Typical of small-town shenanigans, it was obvious that the fire chief was stringing along the chamber director and the lonely, unattached county employee. So why not? He knew she was moving away and wouldn't be here long. The only thing he didn't count on was the perceptive observance of people who live in a small town. Nothing goes unnoticed. And nothing remains unrepeated. Maybe it was a source of entertainment. Only, at the expense of others.

She heard vehicle tires crunch on the gravel and peeped out the office window into the shop bay.

Jack honked as he pulled in. Janie reluctantly swung her boots to the floor and planted a smile on her face. She waved before wiping her hands with a grease rag. Standing at the front of the shop, she motioned for Jack to keep driving forward, and then held up both hands. As he rolled to a stop, she popped the hood.

"Two hundred, huh?" She leaned over the engine.

"Yes, ma'am." Jack got out of his car and stood next to Janie at the front of the SUV.

"I know of a few things to adjust, but is this on the county's dime or out of your pocket? I might have to work on this after hours."

"The sheriff knows all about it. Order whatever parts you need."

181

"I will do my best so that you can catch the bad guys." She laughed.

He turned to face her, one hip leaned against the car. "I'm sorry I had to abandon you on our date. I hope you're not mad."

She avoided him, staring intently under the hood, checking this and that. Her mind went blank on what to say to change the subject.

"What did you and Mack end up doing? Did you go to a movie?"

"No." Janie cleared her throat and glanced up. "Actually, he took me to Sixth Street."

"Wasn't that the weekend of the Harley-Davidson rally?" Wide eyes stared at her in surprise.

"That would be the one. Hand me that ten-millimeter wrench from the bench over there. When's the last time you had your battery changed?"

"I can't believe he took you to that rally. Christy would never agree to that. It's a bit of a rough crowd for a lady," he said from across the shop.

"Actually, it was a really fun event. I met so many interesting people, and we looked at some very unique Harleys."

"*You* like motorcycles?" he asked as he handed her the wrench.

"Yes, I do. Never had enough money to buy one for myself, but I've been obsessed since high school. My dad would have gladly bought me a horse, but motorcycles were not an option."

"The chief likes Harleys too."

"Hummm," was all she said.

He hesitated a minute. "Have you ever been on Mack's Harley?" His tone was soft and disapproving.

Janie bristled. Great. Someone else questioning her

actions. This town was really getting on her last nerve. They weren't involved in any way, and he had no right to ask for a report of what she did. In the big picture of things, did it really matter that she had been on the back of Mack's bike?

"As a matter of fact, I have. Those firefighter editions are something, aren't they?"

"Where'd he take you?"

Janie spun around to face him. "Jack. I appreciate you for inviting me out, but we aren't in an exclusive relationship. In fact, we aren't in a relationship of any kind. So why do I feel like I'm on trial here?"

"We could be." He stepped closer and put both hands on her shoulders. "I want us to be together."

He leaned closer like he was going to kiss her, and she placed her hands on his chest. "No, Jack. I'm sorry."

"Am I interrupting something?" A deep, irritated voice boomed through the shop, making Janie and Jack jump apart. Fury clouded Mack's eyes as he looked from one to the other. "This is highly inappropriate behavior for the workplace."

"I was just leaving as soon as my ride gets here. Ahh, and here it is." Without another word to Janie, and walking a wide berth around the car to avoid Mack, he hurried outside and climbed into the waiting vehicle with the sheriff.

"Nothing is going on," Janie said. "Can I help you?"

"I was just checking if you had time to look at our tanker truck. Remember?"

"I will call you after I get done with Jack's vehicle."

"First names now, is it? So, that's how it's going to be?"

"What do you mean?"

183

"It's all about Jack now, and Saturday night is forgotten?"

She swallowed the lump in her throat. "Saturday night was wonderful. I had a great time, but you have a girlfriend, and you were just supposed to give me a ride home. That was it."

Janie really wanted to recount the scene from the beauty salon, but what good would it do? She'd just be adding to the gossip mill and stirring up more strife between them. She wanted to remember Mack as they were on Saturday. Heads together, completely enthralled in a vintage Harley, amazed at the piece of Americana. It had been a perfect evening.

"I'm sorry I overreacted about the flowers."

"What set you off like that?"

Again, should she tell him about Christy's accusations? He looked at her with curiosity and a bit of sadness. She suspected he knew that he was going to have to deal with both women. Not a popular option for any man.

"I'm not stringing you both along," he said.

"Hummm," she replied and turned back to Jack's car. "I have work to do. I'll call you in a few days."

She watched him walk back towards the firehouse, not taking her eyes off him until he had disappeared inside. Her heart fell to the floor. She had never felt so abandoned. An unexplainable void descended upon her as though she was suddenly all alone in the world. She wanted to go after him. Maybe there was a chance. Surely the connection they had at the rally wasn't fake. She had never experienced a bond like that before, so maybe she wouldn't recognize it and had misunderstood things. But the ugliest girl in town and the handsome fire chief only happened in romance novels, never in her reality.

With a heavy heart and a sigh, she focused her attention on the engine. Life would be much simpler if she just did her job and forgot about socializing. She tugged a purple do-rag from the back pocket of her overalls and tied it on her head.

34
JANIE

Over the next few days Janie successfully stayed hidden in the county mechanic's barn, working on the deputy's vehicle. After work she went straight home to the Rafter O, ran every evening, and helped with chores if there was anything that needed doing.

Her family was abuzz over the Founders' Day celebration and they had talked about nothing else. She was proud that her family was being recognized, but she couldn't help wondering about the names of the other settler families who had taken a chance in the middle of nowhere on a prayer and a promise. Like Mack's family, for instance.

She had also managed to keep a low profile and avoid her sister, Angie, as well. She didn't want any more questions or any conversations that required her to explain why she was back home, when would she be leaving, or if she was going out with Deputy Jack Skinner again. The inquisition that her sister could deliver was exhausting, to say the least.

On Thursday, she had a chance to do research at the library during her lunch break and learned that the town of Dixon had been filled with many devoted citizens, not just the Olsens. She never called Mack about his tanker truck. Honestly, she just didn't have the energy to face him. Besides, Jack's repairs kept her busy enough. The week went by fast, and she finally made it through to Friday.

"We need to talk." The sound of high heels clicking on the cement floor confirmed the fact of who the voice belonged to, even before Janie looked out from behind the hood. Christy.

"I'm actually really busy. Can this wait?" Janie did not look up from her work.

A flurry in a light blue suit and ruffled white blouse accentuated by the scent of warm, soft florals floated into view.

"We need to clear the air between us, now."

Janie sighed and straightened up, bending backwards to stretch her back. "Okay, what is it?"

"Mack's different."

"I never knew him before, and don't really care to understand him now."

"He says you went to high school together, but he doesn't remember you."

No surprise there, but to hear her say it aloud still stung. Janie refused to let the hurt show on her face. Instead, she turned and walked over to the tool bench and pretended to look for something. Anything.

"He won't talk about what happened after Jack and I left to come back to Dixon that night. Why?"

Janie slammed a hammer on the bench and walked closer to Christy. It was time she cleared the record and

187

NATALIE BRIGHT & DENISE F. MCALLISTER

nipped this in the bud. This town was going to cause her to have a nervous breakdown, if she let it. It was the same all over again. The rumors and everybody concerned about each other's business instead of taking care of their own.

"Christy, really. I don't have time for your small-town games and rumors. If you need information, you should really talk to your boyfriend, not me."

"But he's not telling me anything, and I want to know." Her voice raised, anger tinged her cheeks red.

Janie shrugged her shoulders. "Okay, fine, because there's nothing to tell really. We went to Sixth Street, to a Harley-Davidson rally. We drank lemonade and ate fried pig skins. We listened to music and talked to other bike riders. Nothing else happened."

The girl stood poised and still, balancing on her high heels without moving. Her head hung to her chest as she stared at the floor. When she slowly raised it, Janie noticed tears brimming her eyes.

"You like stuff like that?" she asked, her voice breaking with emotion.

"Actually, yes. I've been a Harley fan most of my life."

"I would never go to anything like that with Mack, even though he's asked me dozens of times. I made a huge mistake, and now I've lost him."

"He is still completely devoted to you. It wasn't a big deal. Believe me. We walked down the middle of a street and looked at parked Harley-Davidson bikes. There's nothing else to tell, Christy. There's nothing for you to worry about."

"You may think it's nothing, but in truth, it's everything."

She wiped a tear from her cheek and turned, stepping

gingerly through the gravel on her heels and walking across the street. Janie watched her. Christy strutted past the fire station without even a second glance and crossed the street again to disappear into the chamber office.

35

JANIE

JANIE BOUNDED INTO THE KITCHEN WEARING
her running shorts and the official race T-shirt she had
picked up the day before at registration.

"You want some coffee and eggs?" her mother asked.

"No, Mom, thanks. I'll just grab a banana and
water."

Grace Olsen had rounded up most of her family for
an early breakfast and even had partial control over the
toddler and baby, who took turns screaming, crying, or
throwing toys. It was a challenge. Janie was amazed at
how her mother kept her cool in the eye of a storm. All
of her siblings were gathered in the kitchen to discuss
last-minute details for the day's events.

Janie's dad sipped his coffee and visited with Angie,
his ranchy daughter. "What time do you need to get the
horses to the parade site?"

"Soon. The race starts at nine. After we watch Janie
run, we'll get right on the horses for the parade, which
starts around 10:30, but you know how loose the
schedule can be in our town," Angie answered. "Too

much standing around jawing, which keeps everyone distracted."

"Nathan, you and Travis gonna help her?"

"Yes, Dad," they both said.

"I only have to load three horses, Pa. I can do that by myself." Then Angie added, "One of the hands volunteered. Logan is coming with us to stay with the trailer."

Grace interjected. "We won't make it to church, but I'm sure the Good Lord won't mind if we read some Scripture and have a prayer at home before we go. Your father and I will take the little ones and all their gear to the race and parade and we'll look for y'all. We'll be right behind the fire truck. They've asked your dad to be the Grand Marshal."

Janie rolled her eyes. Her mother had only mentioned that a hundred times in the past few days.

"Okay, thanks, Mom," Nathan said. To his little boy, he added, "And you be a good boy for grandma and papa. Okay?"

Gabriel nodded. "K, Dada."

"Nathan, where is Indya? She's riding with us in the parade, isn't she?"

"Yes, ma'am. She'll meet you there at the parade route."

Travis placed the camouflage-patterned baby carrier on the counter. "Don't forget Wyatt's flak jacket."

Everyone laughed. But his mother said, "He's such a cute little thing. I miss the old days of Nemo and Winnie the Pooh. And what about Destynee?"

"I'm not sure where my wife is." Her youngest son grumbled, but his face lit up with a smile when he looked at his son. "As far as this guy goes, we gotta make him into a little man."

Grace shook her head. "Janie, have you decided to

ride with Angie and the boys on a horse, or do you want to ride with us in the truck?"

"I don't know. They'll be busy with the horses. Maybe I should just take my car." If she rode a horse, then she'd have to take her boots and jeans, and find somewhere to change after the race. It seemed like a lot of trouble for a few minutes.

Angie gulped her coffee and filled a stainless-steel mug with more. "We're about to leave any minute. Why not come with us? Logan will stay with the trailer so I don't have to do anything when we get there. I can wait with you before the race."

"All right, I guess so," Janie said. "I just don't want to be late."

"We won't make you late. So, let's hurry up and hit the road." Angie tightened the lid on her coffee.

Skip cleared his throat and in a loud voice commanded attention in the room. "Now just a minute. Did y'all forget something?"

They all stared at him, but his wife smiled and passed the Bible to him on the counter.

He opened his dog-eared, marked-up copy and began to read.

"Isaiah 40, verses 28 to 31.

> 'Do you not know? Have you not heard?
> The Lord is the everlasting God, the Creator of the
>   ends of the earth.
> He will not grow tired or weary, and his under-
>   standing no one can fathom.
> He gives strength to the weary and increases the
>   power of the weak.
> Even youths grow tired and weary, and young
>   men stumble and fall;

but those who hope in the Lord will renew their
*   strength.*
They will soar on wings like eagles; they will run
*   and not grow weary,*
they will walk and not be faint.'

"I chose that verse for Janie because of the last lines. But it applies to all of us." He winked at his daughter. "Let's pray," he continued. Everyone bowed their heads.

"Dear God, please watch over all of us today. Protect my kids as they're driving to the celebration, riding the horses in the parade, and Janie as she runs the race. Please bless all of the people who come to the event. Help them to recognize and accept you as Lord of their lives. For we are not in control. That's your job, and you only want the best for us. In Jesus's name, we pray. Amen."

The entire Olsen clan responded. "Amen."

"Go on now. We'll be right behind you," Grace said to her kids. "Let's get a good spot on the street so we can watch Janie's race."

THE OLSEN SIBLINGS had kissed their folks, stormed out the door, loaded the horses, and were on their way all within a few minutes. Janie was between Logan and Travis in the backseat of the Rafter O dually truck, which pulled the gooseneck trailer. Angie drove with Nathan in the shotgun seat. Her parents had both grandsons bringing up the rear of their caravan. They had spent most of Saturday brushing down horses, and they had washed and detailed her father's pickup truck for the parade.

Janie couldn't help but remember her brothers and sisters at different ages—pre-teens as they invented adventures together on the ranch, teenagers as they took an interest in the opposite sex, and now. Her brothers married with sons of their own. They all had a purpose and seemed happy and settled.

What was she going to do with the rest of her life? She'd have to make some tough decisions soon. Maybe move away from Dixon. Do something completely different from her family. Invent a brand-new life for herself. See the world.

As Janie daydreamed, Angie drove them to town and pulled the truck and trailer into the parking lot of the United Methodist Church, where the parade participants gathered.

The volunteer noted Angie's name as a parade entry on a clipboard and pointed her to an empty grassy area. "You can park over there. I'm supposed to remind everyone about the parade route. We'll start here at this end of town, proceed along Main Street to the other end of town, and then you'll turn and go one block over, proceed along First Street, and end up back here. Got it?"

"Yes, ma'am. Thank you." Angie smiled, buzzed her window up, and then mumbled, "It's not like they have any other choice of parade routes in this town. They've done that same route for fifty years."

Janie laughed and nodded in agreement.

The truck jostled over some uneven mounds and then came to a rest. Angie turned off the ignition. "I guess this'll have to do. It's not too far away from where the parade starts."

They all got out and readied themselves to head towards Main Street and find a place to watch the race. Nathan, Travis, and Angie were dressed in their starched shirts for the parade. They would come back to the trailer to get the horses when the time was right. Angie gave instructions to the ranch hand to stay with the trailer.

"Thanks, Logan," Angie called out. "We'll be back after Janie's run."

As the four of them walked towards the event site, Janie's heart skipped a beat when she spotted the fire engine and Mack's truck. A medical vehicle was parked in a designated spot to be on hand for the race, just in case of an injury.

Her heart and her head were in a constant battle now. This couldn't go on much longer without her losing her mind. She had envisioned a brief and peaceful time spent with her family until she figured out her next move. She hadn't even imagined someone like Mack coming into her life. I've got to figure out what to do with the rest of my life. And I've got to figure out about *him*.

36
JANIE

"ARE YOU ALL SET, JANIE? DID YOU GET registered at the table?"

Her sister, Angie, really was helpful to her, no matter how much they kidded back and forth, and she over-thought everything, just like their mother. And Janie was grateful, but she was more of a roll-with-the-flow type of person, figure it out as you go. That had always driven her sister crazy.

Her mind drifted to Mack. She spotted him earlier near the fire truck, probably getting ready for the parade after the race, but they hadn't spoken. She didn't really want to talk to anyone. She'd rather hide and get her mind ready to run. But she came out for this celebration because her mother had asked her and her siblings to participate, and because running was involved. Maybe she had been running her whole life in a lot of ways.

"What?" She had no idea what Angie had just said to her.

"Earth to Janie. I just wanted to check that you have everything."

"Yeah, I registered yesterday and picked up my T-shirt and number."

"There's a porta-potty right over there if you need it. I'll hang on to your jacket and water."

"Okay. I'll be right back."

"I'll be waiting." Angie smiled, holding her arms out like a ballerina.

It was sunny that morning and Janie wore wraparound sunglasses. She didn't want to make eye contact with anyone. She was probably the talk of the town by now. Maybe even labeled as the other woman. Christy had a way of sharing news, otherwise known to most people as gossip. It was difficult to go unnoticed and keep your life private in the small town of Dixon.

There was a little bit of a line at the portable toilet. If it hadn't been for all the water she consumed, she would have rather skipped this creepy closet and prayed it would not tip over with her in it. While she waited for some junior high kids in front of her, she listened to their conversation.

Three smart-alecky boys were in the line waiting for the porta-potty on the left, a gangly girl with a frizzy ponytail stood directly in front of Janie, and a pretty girl was ahead of her, next to enter the latrine.

"Are those bird legs gonna hold you up, Linda Binda?"

"Don't fall down in front of me in the race. I'll jump right over ya."

The boys broke out in laughter and shoved each other. The girl in front of Janie only stared at the ground.

And the pretty girl, whose training bra appeared to be stuffed with something, smiled at the boys as she stuck out her chest and flipped her long hair over her shoulder.

"Now y'all leave her alone. She can't help it."

The first boy was nearly licking his lips as though the pretty girl was a beauty queen. Or an ice cream cone. "No, she can't help that you're so beautiful, Patty."

Boy number two chimed in with, "Patty Perfect."

Boy three had to get in on the action too, it seemed. "Yeah, Linda Binda, don't blow away on those stick legs. You might fly away to the next county."

"That'd be a good thing. Fly away, Linda Binda," the first boy said, deepening his voice, then flapping his arms like a bird and squawking.

That was it. It reminded Janie too much of her youth. She leaned towards the girl. "Is your name Linda?"

The girl nodded and kept her glistening eyes guarded.

"And you like to run?"

Again, a nod.

"Well, let me tell you something, Linda, which is a pretty name, by the way. I like to run too, and I'll bet you'll be a great runner. And even if you don't win today, you will win someday. I had a hard time in school. But you know what? I grew up and I did okay. Boys like that used to make fun of me too. And those boys who made fun of me?"

Janie glared at the trouble-making juveniles who were standing at attention now. "Those stupid jerk boys probably grew up to be stupid jerk men. And I could whip them all with one hand tied behind my back."

Her wrath was almost palpable as it spewed all over the boys who appeared to cower in their new, diminished stature. "Sorry, ma'am," one of them said.

"You should be apologizing to Linda here. And if I ever hear of any of you making jokes at her expense, just remember, I will come after you. And your parents and principal will hear about it. You got that?"

The boys all said, "Yes, ma'am," and "Sorry, Linda."

Janie wasn't done yet.

Right before the pretty girl got to the porta-potty, Janie called to her, "And, Patty, you shouldn't flaunt your beauty. A woman with genuine beauty will help and defend another woman, not contribute to her unhappiness."

The girl said, "Sorry," and quickly opened the door to the bathroom and disappeared inside.

Janie was embarrassed at her outburst but smiled politely. And then told Linda, "Good luck. Have fun."

She had to get out of there. She'd find another toilet or run into a store across the street. Or duck behind a tree if she had to.

As she was making her getaway, she noticed Christy with a clipboard, tugging Mack along, her mouth moving a mile a minute. Mack glanced at Janie and their eyes locked for a brief moment, but then he turned away and kept walking.

After Janie found another porta john, she made her way back to Angie.

"Gosh, it took you long enough. I got worried. You okay?"

"I'm fine. Let's just say I had to take care of some punks." Janie gave a half-smile.

"You're not gonna get arrested, are you?"

"No. But they might be someday."

"Well, you need to get to the front of the line. The race is about to start. They let the fastest runners go to the front, walkers in the back."

"Angie, I've done this before. Many times."

"Oh, right."

Janie rolled her eyes, but also smiled at her sister. She turned to walk away. "Guess I'll see you at the finish."

"We'll all be there. Mom and Dad, Nathan, and Travis.

"Everyone?"

"Of course. We want to see you win. You'd better win! Uphold the family name and all that." Angie playfully balled up her fist and shook it at Janie. "Wait'll you see Travis wearing his new baby carrier. And Nathan with the stroller for Gabriel. It's kinda funny to see them as dads."

"Yeah, it is."

Before she left to gather at the start with the other runners, Angie stopped her again.

"Janie, run your heart out. Forget all about what's happened in the last few days. This race is for you. I know running is your happy place. So, enjoy yourself."

"Thanks, Sis."

Those old adages were true. Family was important. They were the people who cared about you no matter what.

37
JANIE

SURROUNDED BY MOSTLY MEN, AND SOME women, Janie got into position towards the front of the runners, those who had marked fast times on their entry form. Whether true times or not, they were at the front of the pack. The starting line would be turned into the finish line on the other side of the blocked-off street.

"Yay, Janie!" a voice called out.

She found a face on the sidelines, her brother Nathan, with a wide grin. Just like when they were kids, he loved teasing her.

Embarrassed, she shook her head but gave him a grin too. Looking down at her white legs, she felt even more self-conscious. Usually, they were concealed under mechanic's coveralls, and running in the early morning or late at night did not afford the sun's help with tanning. She was glad her upper body caught some rays though, and her muscular toned arms looked pretty good.

The group was full of excitement and raring to be

unleashed. A couple of men nudged her but did not apologize as they kept their own focus.

Only three and a half miles. She did more than that on a daily basis. Piece of cake. It was all in the name of fun, for charity.

"Okay, runners, get ready. Wait for the gun. Be careful and have a good race."

A man's voice came over the megaphone. She had almost expected to hear Christy's after all her showboating about running the day's event.

The gun sounded, and the throng moved, compact at first like one entity, then breaking up into individual cells.

Janie could feel the familiar rhythm of her shoes hitting the pavement. She was about to start her running mantra. It wouldn't be one of the Army's cadence songs. Hers would be borrowed from famous runners she had read about—calm, calm, calm, relax, relax, relax, focus, focus, focus, I am a runner, I am a runner. Sometimes she'd resort to simple multiplication tables or counting— two times two is four, four times two is eight, eight times two is sixteen, sixteen times two is thirty-two.

She was carving out her path away from the others. As she passed, she noticed their different shapes and ages. Some men with jiggly paunches, and either too tight shorts or droopy bottoms, who were obviously just in it for the fun. One held an unlit cigar in his mouth and elbowed his friend. He wore Cat in the Hat headgear. Perhaps they had started their partying early, or it was left over from the night before.

A few other guys looked familiar, city employees she'd met, family friends from neighboring ranches, and some of Mack's firefighting crew. She knew he was here, she'd spotted him earlier near the porta john. With Christy.

Put him out of your mind. Just run. He's got his life, you've got yours. Don't get distracted.

Mile two. Runners were thinning out. One of the firefighters caught up next to her and nodded. Janie smiled. At this rate, she might even win this thing.

She was gliding effortlessly and watched the people on the sidelines. Her hometown. They all had their lives. Marriages. Kids in school. Church. She envied them in a way. They knew what they wanted, and they were living. She was still searching. For what? Tell me, God. Show me what I'm supposed to do with my life.

Three miles. She was feeling clear-minded, almost euphoric. She loved running.

In her peripheral vision, a small figure with frizzy brown hair emerged next to her.

"Linda? Have you run all this way? How old are you?"

The girl smiled. "Thirteen. I was trying to catch you."

"Wow, I'm impressed. Look at you go, girl. You feeling okay?"

"I'm fine."

"Well, let's do this thing. We're almost at the finish."

They talked, but both were a little winded.

The firefighter was still alongside and smiled at her and the girl. "Nice work," he said.

Just as they were approaching the finish line, the cigar-wielding clown rushed up with a temporary burst of adrenaline and bumped into Linda. "Look out, kid, this race is for grownups." His cronies bumped into him laughing, and down went Linda.

Wanting to shield the girl, Janie stopped as the pileup took her down too, catapulting her into a sideways somersault. "Hey, watch out." she cried to the doltish men who feigned apologies in between laughter.

Janie and Linda rose from their prone positions and sat up on the asphalt, blood trickling down their legs. The finish line was so close, Janie could have crawled across it. They had been inches away from winning. Disappointment was overshadowed by her concern for the young girl.

"Are you okay, Linda?" Janie leaned closer to her and surveyed the damage. It wasn't a deep cut, more like a scrape, but it was bleeding. Droplets had stained the pavement. She couldn't believe the girl wasn't crying. She didn't notice the blood on her own knees.

"Yeah, it just stings."

The firefighter who had been next to them earlier had gained ground when Janie met up with Linda. He rushed through the finish line and then, noticing the commotion behind him, came back. Wearing part of his gear to pay homage to his firefighting family, he pushed the call button on his shoulder radio. "Need assistance at the finish line, downed runners."

He helped the girls to the side of the road to allow for other runners to pass, and a volunteer quickly appeared with water bottles.

Janie put a hand on Linda's shoulder, who was tearing up. "Hey, it's okay. We were really close. Who do you think would've been first? You or me?"

The girl smiled a little and said, "You."

"I don't know, Linda. I think you were about to take over the lead."

She heard a beeping and whoop-whoop sound of an emergency vehicle, and suddenly, a deep voice was above her.

"Did someone call for assistance? We heard two winners were robbed of their first-place ribbons."

Mack grinned down at her, and she saw compassion and a look of concern filling his eyes. "Are you all right?"

She couldn't find any words as he wiped an alcohol swab across her knee and down her shin. The other firefighter did the same with Linda as he assessed her scrapes.

Mustering her voice, Janie said, "I think we're fine. Thank you."

"Well, I only have one question for you," Mack said.

Oh, goodness, she wondered what it was. She stared up at him and looked into the face she wanted so badly to touch.

"Do you want a Little Mermaid band-aid or Olaf?"

Janie laughed. No matter how awkward or serious the situation, Mack could always diffuse it and make her feel special. She lost herself for a brief moment in the depths of his dark eyes, and then wondered if Christy felt this special too. She pushed his hands away to break the trance.

"I'm fine," she said.

A volunteer tapped the firefighter on his shoulder. "Here's your medal. You came in first."

He shook his head. "That doesn't go to me. I think this belongs to you." He handed the medal to Linda and winked at Janie.

The young girl's mouth hung open and she stuttered. "But that's yours. You came in first."

The firefighter rested a hand on her shoulder. "I have a feeling you were going to be in the lead. And if it hadn't been for those yahoos who ran into you, I'm sure you would have crossed the finish line first." He looked at Janie. "Don't you agree?"

Janie almost teared up, but Mack was still close by, and she wanted to maintain her composure. "I whole-heartedly agree. Linda, you are a champion. No doubt about it."

The little girl's smile covered her face and Janie was sure she had forgotten all about her scraped-up legs.

Janie stood to give Linda a congratulatory hug and then realized her mistake. Pain shot through her ankle and up her leg. "Owwww."

Mack was immediately at her side to lend a supporting arm. The pain miraculously subsided as she leaned into his protective warmth. She could get used to this safe spot in his arms. The knowledge made her even more sad because he kept whittling away at her resolve to not become involved.

"Linda! Linda! Are you all right?" A woman was soon by her side, hugging her tightly.

"Look, Mom! I won."

"You sure did. And I am so proud of you."

38
JANIE

THE OLSEN PARENTS HAD MADE THEIR WAY, with baby boys in tow, down to the sidewalk where Janie and the young runner, Linda, were being treated for their scrapes. Gabriel's mother and Nathan's wife, Indya, had joined them too. They all gathered around Janie, concern on their faces.

"Are you okay, Janie?" her mother asked.

"We're fine, Mom. Don't worry." She looked at her young friend and smiled at the girl's mother who was beside her.

"Angie and your brothers had to hurry to the trailer and get the horses ready. The parade will start soon after all the walkers finish. Do you want to ride with your father and me in the ranch truck?"

Janie looked at the firefighter who had helped them, then scanned the crowd. She needed to thank Mack.

As if he could read her mind, the young man said, "Chief Mack had to get back to our crew for the start of the parade. I can stick around if you need anything."

"That's okay. We're fine. Thanks for all your help. And the medal too. That was really kind of you."

"No problem. My pleasure."

"Janie?" her mother had not gotten an answer yet.

"Sure, Mom, I'll ride with you."

The firefighter helped Janie to her feet and gave Linda a hug before he took off. He shook Linda's mother's hand, who looked like she was about to cry. He invited them to the firehouse whenever they wanted.

Janie never saw where the grown men who had run into them ended up. No apologies. They just disappeared into the crowd. It was hard to figure out why people do or don't do certain things. Were they remorseful and hiding in shame? Had they really been partying and didn't want to get in trouble? Or maybe they were adult men with attitudes like children? Like those boys at the porta john? Just having fun at the expense of others.

Her life was already complicated and difficult to figure out. She didn't have the strength to contemplate other people's lives and motives.

Almost on cue, a piercing, upbeat voice interrupted her musings. Christy.

First, Janie heard the voice. Then as she walked with her mother towards their vehicle, she saw Christy standing on a flatbed truck decorated with red, white, and blue bunting. Dressed in a flowered, spring dress with yellow heels, her hair was poofed up for the occasion. She raised the megaphone to her mouth.

"Ladies and Gentlemen! Welcome to Dixon's Founders' Day celebration! Thank y'all for coming out on this beautiful Sunday. We appreciate every one of you. There will be lots of fun events for you and your family to enjoy throughout the day. We just concluded the 5K race, that was very exciting. I just received a note that there was a little mix-up at the finish, but we got it straightened out, and now I would like to announce that Miss Linda La Barinda was the winner. And, y'all, she's only thirteen years old! Congratulations to Linda! She will receive a twenty-five-dollar gift certificate to the Curl Up & Dye beauty shop! Get yourself a mani-pedi, girl-friend!" Christy giggled and scrunched her shoulders playfully as though telling a secret. "It's never too early to start a girl on pampering."

She cleared her throat and gave another giant smile. "Next up will be our parade featuring many of our local businesses, the school band, horses, and of course, our volunteer fire department! Be sure to show your appreci-ation for every entry. Throughout the day, you'll have many choices of yummy food to try. Bar-b-que, hot dogs and hamburgers, ice cream, cotton candy, funnel cakes. You name it. We've got it! There are a few bouncy houses, face painting, and a dunk tank. It'll be a great day! And later this evening, we'll be awarding a special plaque to outstanding citizens of Dixon! You don't want to miss any of it! Now I don't want to keep jabbering on and on. I'll just say, thank you for being here today. Thank you to our many sponsors. And let's get this party started with our parade. It'll go down Main Street, so find your spot now. The parade will start in a few minutes!"

~

GRACE OLSEN PUSHED Gabriel in his stroller and her husband toted the sleeping baby, Wyatt, across his chest in the flak jacket, as they called it, to the truck.

"C'mon, Janie. How do your legs feel? You okay?" Always the mother, Grace would forever be concerned about her children, no matter how old they got. Janie loved her for it, but she had other things to deal with at the moment.

"I'm fine, Mom. It barely hurts," she said. Although her ankle was still throbbing, she tried not to favor it when her mother was watching. They'd have to find a bandage and ointment, and it would turn into a whole other thing.

When they got closer to their truck, Janie noticed that someone had decorated it with several banners which read, SKIP OLSEN PARADE MARSHAL.

"That's so nice," Grace said. "Look at that, Janie."

Janie reached for the baby bag Grace held. "Let me help you. Give me Gabe and you can fold up the stroller."

"I guess you're driving, Janie." Skip fastened sleeping Wyatt into his car seat.

Janie greeted her sister-in-law who waited by the truck. "Indya. It's so good to finally meet you. And congratulations on the upcoming baby."

Indya returned the hug and then patted her tummy. "We are excited. Finally, we meet. I'm sorry I haven't been out to the house."

"I hear your gallery is doing well, and Gabriel is such a precious little boy. I've enjoyed watching him." Janie was happy for Nathan, and she liked Indya immediately.

Indya helped Grace with the stroller before they all piled into the white truck, the Rafter O brand emblazoned on both sides. Janie stopped to admire the truck with their brand and the banners. A sense of pride made her happy that she had come back home. It was good to be involved in this event.

Once they got settled into the truck and both boys were secured in their car seats, Janie made a quick count of heads to make sure they had everyone. Gabriel fussed a bit, but Janie calmed him down with smiles and tickles. Luckily, he was smitten with her.

Mrs. Olsen looked at her husband, who still wore the flak jacket. "Are you gonna keep that thing on? Who's going to drive?"

He laughed. "Sure I am. We're best buds, little Wyatt and me. In case he wakes up, I'll be holding him if he starts fussing."

"I'm driving, Mother. You can get in the back with the boys." They had buckled in both car seats next to the windows, and Grace squeezed in between. Indya rode in the middle up front with Skip and Janie. Thank goodness for oversized cab trucks. Janie opened the door and got behind the wheel. If she'd known that her parents needed a driver, she would have bought bags of candy to throw.

The megaphone sounded from down the street with Christy's voice. "Ladies and Gentlemen! Welcome again to Dixon's Founders' Day. I hope everyone has found a place on the street. Please remember to be careful and don't go in front of the vehicles as they pass. Relax, wave, and have a great time, y'all! Here we go. Let's get started. First, please place your hands on your hearts for our National Anthem. Then our brave firefighters will start the parade. They freely volunteer their time to protect us, and we appreciate all they do."

Music played the National Anthem and the crowd grew silent.

Janie swallowed and her stomach fluttered when the fire engine rolled past. Of course, she looked for him. He had been very gentle when he cleaned off her bloody, scraped knees, and she was thrilled to have him close. They didn't really have an opportunity to talk, but his eyes spoke volumes, yet she was always left undone when he was anywhere around her.

Just then, the fire engine blasted its horn and the sirens screamed.

Little Gabriel put his tiny hands over his ears and squealed, but his smiling face was full of excitement. Then he started to cry. Grace covered baby Wyatt's ears with her palms and the baby never awoke.

"Unbuckle Gabe, Mom, and hand him up here. He can sit in my lap until it's our turn to pull into the parade route."

Janie soothed her nephew. "You're all right Gabe. Look at the fire trucks."

They watched the engine drive by in the lead, an American flag affixed to its tail end. She held on to Gabe's legs as he pointed and bounced with excitement in her lap. And then Mack passed by on that glorious red Harley-Davidson. Even though he was waving, she did not wave back, and for a few very long seconds, they made eye contact and held it. What difference would it make if they were friends or not? She wouldn't be here that much longer.

"I think we go after the fire trucks," her father said.

"Are you sure? Actually, the Grand Marshal should have gone first."

"The money raised today will go to the fire station, so they want the volunteers to be seen and heard apparently," Grace added.

Janie helped Gabriel crawl back to his car seat while Grace buckled him in.

The audience clapped as the vehicles passed, and she couldn't help herself from raising a hand to wave at the firemen after Mack had gone past. A capable group of volunteers that she had grown to love. After a long line of fire department vehicles went by, including plain ranch trucks with volunteers inside, Janie pulled into the street behind the line of fire department equipment.

In her rearview mirror, she saw a long red convertible that might've belonged to Miss Hattie or one of the other elderly residents. A banner was attached to both sides and front of the car with balloons tied to the antenna. They honked.

"Janie! Janie!" Karmelle hung from the driver's side window yelling her name, and Chimmi waved from the passenger seat. She smiled and raised a hand. "It's the Curl Up sisters."

Janie could only see their top halves in the car, but it looked like Chimmi wore a purple outfit with fringe-trimmed sleeves that swung as she waved. Karmelle had something bright pink on, which was very uncharacteristic for her style.

"Chimmi must've picked out their outfits," Janie said with a giggle.

As she crept along at ten miles an hour, she looked in her rearview mirror, and Janie saw that following the Curl Up sisters was a blue SUV which belonged to Belinda and her husband, Russell, from the B&R Beanery. It was good to see the local businesses participating in the parade.

It was dawning on Janie how many people she knew in their small town, and they were all becoming good friends. What would it be like to go to a brand-new place where she was a total stranger? And have to start over. Without her family. Without Mack.

Continuing on at a snail's pace, both sides of the street were lined with people. Janie smiled and waved, and wished they had candy to throw. There were many calls and shouts for her dad. That made her happy that she was able to share this day with her family.

At the opposite end of Main Street from where they began, Janie slowed to a stop. The lead fire truck turned right, but the next fire engine turned left. This was something new. She racked her brains to try to remember if the volunteer had been more specific in the parade route, but she couldn't remember.

"Do you know which way, Dad?" she asked.

"Doesn't matter," he said. "Looks like there are people on both sides of the street either way."

She made the decision to follow the lead fire engine, picking up her speed a bit to catch up. Her father kept waving and she stared straight ahead, glancing down the side streets to see the other parade entries moving in the opposite direction a block away. As they got closer to where they had begun at the Methodist Church parking lot, Janie pulled over and stopped to allow the others to pass them. They had a good view. There were several more businesses who had floats, and a long line of antique tractors. Gabriel spied them out his window, which thrilled him to no end as they chugged past.

Children on decorated bikes, a group of dogs on leashes led by various sizes of kids, a few men painted up like clowns, and more floats from area businesses. And last were the horses, which was their position every year. She saw her siblings, Nathan, Angie, and Travis, starting off the procession. Wearing their cowboy hats, spurs, white shirts, and best saddles, they definitely shined. There was something for everybody.

In front of them walked a couple of kids they had given a few bucks to for carrying a sign. Olsen Family.

Janie grinned and said to her mother, "I didn't know they were going to have a sign."

"Well, sure. How would you know who they were?"

"Uh, Mom, I think people know who they are."

Janie held two fingers in her mouth and whistled loudly. Nathan heard the familiar sound he had taught her, looked up and waved.

The horses clip-clopped by, followed by other groups of riders, some holding Texas flags and others wearing coordinated outfits. Janie swelled with pride. Never thought my little hometown could pull off such a big event.

MACK

MACK HAD WAVED EARLIER TO JANIE AS HE drove past on his bike, but she did not wave back. He wondered what she was thinking because she had not avoided his eyes. A baby was on her lap and she was driving the Grand Marshal of the parade, Skip Olsen. Clearly friends of the family because she was always with their daughter, Angie Olsen. Seemed like a lot of people in Dixon liked her. He knew she saw him. She looked sweet holding that baby. Maybe he'd have kids someday. He'd like that.

Glad the parade was over, he joined his crew around their vehicles, which were still parked in the church parking lot at the beginning of the parade route.

"Good job, guys. I think people liked seeing the department."

As they exchanged high-fives and pats on the back, a female voice entered the space along with the clickity-click of heels.

If he were honest with himself, the sound of her voice

grated on his nerves and had become an irritant. Maybe it was time to be honest.

"Y'all did great, thank you so much! That was an awesome parade. Now, if I may, I'd like to speak with my boyfriend for just a little minute. I've got to get back to my duties right quick. This thing ain't over yet! Thanks again, guys! I really appreciate all that you do. Mack, can I have a word?"

He didn't like her saying "boyfriend". And he didn't like the way she said it.

She tugged his arm, leading him away from the men.

"What do you want, Christy? I need to get this equipment out of the street and back into the firehouse."

"Is there somewhere we can sit and chat for a minute?" She giggled that giggle of hers.

"We can stand here. I don't have time to go back inside." He led her away from the men to where they stood, in the shade at the side of the church building. She was a nice girl, pretty too. But why was she bugging him so much now?

He suspected it might be because of Janie. And he couldn't help himself. He was drawn to Janie. A casual acquaintance wasn't enough for him. Not now.

"Now, Mack, I have felt for a while that we needed to talk." She made it sound like the start of a business meeting, and he wouldn't be surprised if she suddenly pulled out a pen and notepad. He'd listen and he'd be kind. He owed her that, at least.

"And it has to be today, at this minute?" He crossed his arms over his chest.

"I just feel we are growing apart. I'm sure you feel it too. You didn't call me that night when you got home after the double-date. You haven't returned my calls yesterday or this morning."

"We've both been busy, Christy. You know that. I've been busy with this parade. The parade that you asked me to work on."

"You and *Jane* went off, and I hear tell that you were out till after midnight."

"Her name is Janie. And I thought you said you'd call me after investigating the break-in at the chamber office."

She appeared a little flushed. "Well, I don't remember who should have called whom."

Mack watched her mouth form an "O" when she stretched out the word "whom" like she was putting on airs.

"The phone call doesn't matter." She continued. "I've been watching you and *Jane*. You don't look at me like that, Mack. I've just got to ask, do you have a thing for her?"

He almost choked, but he was glad to have it out in the open. This was a turning point, and he had to seize it.

A thing? Fine. If that's what you call it. "Yes, I do."

She was the one to cough. "Well, honey, don't sugar-coat it for me."

He watched her almost feign tears, but she stopped and straightened her spine and lifted her chin.

"Christy, you are a sweet girl, a beautiful girl. And I appreciate our friendship. But lately, it's been dawning on me that that is what it is. A good friendship. I am comfortable with you. We have a good working relationship. I know we've dated for a while, but I'm not in love with you. I'm sorry."

"Are you in love with her?"

"I really care about her. I don't know if it's love."

"Well, I've got my answer then. But I want you to

know something, Mack. You are not dumping me. I have big plans. I'm going places with the chamber of this town and beyond. People respect me. And I get lots of dating requests. I'm talking about lots! Every day some man asks me out." She took a breath, then added, "And I will not lower myself to diss another woman, but I truly do not understand what you see in *Plain Jane*. For goodness sakes, she wears overalls and she has grease under her fingernails."

He smiled. "And she also likes the same things that I do. And Christy, her name is Janie."

"Whatever." Christy walked away, then turned to look at him. "I've got to go. You know I'm in charge. This day would have never happened without me, and it isn't over yet. I'd better get back to work."

Mack followed her and touched her arm. "Christy, wait. Still friends?"

She turned and squinted at him as though she was about to chastise him like a schoolteacher. Instead, she grinned and patted his cheek. "Mack, we'll always be friends. Take care. I truly wish you all the best with your new girlfriend, but she's *Plain Jane*, and that's all she'll ever be. You deserve better."

Mack didn't argue, but he knew deep down that there was much more to Janie. He chuckled to himself. He really should find out her last name.

40
MACK

MACK JOINED HIS MEN AS THEY WAITED NEAR the trucks. He made assignments for drivers and they formed a caravan back towards the garages after the parade. The men hung around the fire station for several hours while Mack shuffled papers in his office and pretended to look busy. He didn't feel like talking.

He and Christy were no longer together. Wonder how long it would take for the word to spread through town? The strangest part about it, he wasn't that upset. Guilt crept into his consciousness, but then he realized she hadn't shed any tears over it. She had tried, but even Christy couldn't fake misery over the break-up. Obviously, her feelings had been the same as his.

The first thing he thought about doing was to find Janie and tell her. He could ask her out on a proper date and get a proper kiss, and they wouldn't be sneaking around. Truthfully, being with Janie never felt wrong. She tormented his mind every second. The way she walked, the sound of her voice, her deep chuckle as opposed to that girly giggle that he thought he liked. The way she smelled.

He had to take things slow though. He sensed she was cautious and not easily trusting of men, which made him even more curious. It was his own driving need that motivated him. He'd never met anyone like her before.

"Aren't you going to the banquet?" One of the men stuck his head through the doorway.

"What time is it?" Mack stood with alarm and noticed he had only thirty minutes to shower, find his suit, and get to the fellowship hall at the Catholic Church. "Gotta go. You boys lock up."

MACK WALKED into the fellowship hall that had been transformed into a time capsule. Christy had outdone herself.

Sofa-sized black and white photographs capturing the early days of Dixon hung on the walls around the room. Various front-page headlines had been blown up as posters to depict the news events over the past decades. He glanced at them as he walked past, but froze in front of one picture with a fire engine. His father was driving one of the vintage fire trucks, and he, as a small boy, stood in the back with one arm raised in a wave, a wide grin on his face. He must have been ten years old. The emotion that tightened his chest from seeing his father's face surprised him. That had been so long ago.

He turned and continued to look over the room, shocked at the transformation. Round tables with elegant black tablecloths, gold candles burned in the centers, surrounded by white roses.

"Mack," Christy said. "You're at the head table."

He blinked and took a second look. "This is nice, and you look stunning." Of course, Christy had to match the decor. She wore a gold floor-length gown, her blonde hair straight and shiny.

"Thank you, but you don't have any right to comment on how I look, so keep your opinions to yourself." Without a friendly smile, which was completely out of character for her, she left him standing alone at the front of the room. He would give her a pass on that one. He knew her. She might pretend to be devastated because he had dumped her, but in a few days, she would be back on top, dominating and outshining everyone in the room.

Not feeling much like being chatty, Mack stayed to himself and continued to look at the historical photos. Early residents and storefronts, long since gone with time, but it reminded him how important everyone's contribution is to the success of a community. It takes all kinds, doing their job and living their lives. Another particular photo caught his attention. It looked like his father again, but when he took a closer look, he realized it must be his great-great-grandfather as a young man. The resemblance to him and his own father was uncanny. A group of people clustered together in front of the mercantile. The inscription on the photo read, *Founding Citizens, 1917, Dixon.*

"Anyone you know?"

He knew that scent and that smooth, deep-throated voice. Mack's senses came alive, and he was afraid to look at her because she might leave. He didn't want to scare her away.

"I believe that's my great-great-grandfather," he muttered without looking in her direction.

Janie leaned forward for a closer look, her nearness

warmed his side, and their arms touched as she peered at the photograph.

"That's interesting, because that's my great-great-grandfather right there."

He looked at her in surprise. "No kidding?" He should have stared straight ahead. She certainly did not look like any mechanic he'd ever known. She wore a red dress that hugged her figure, with a wide neckline that exposed her perfect shoulders. He couldn't tear his gaze away.

"Wow!" was all that he could manage to say.

"It's my sister's dress." She laughed. "I don't own anything like this."

"Now, which one is your great-great-grandfather?" He turned his attention back to the photograph, otherwise he'd have to scoop her up in his arms and find the nearest exit. She needed to be kissed looking like that.

"That one. I think that's Lars Olsen. He's the one closest to your relative."

"You're an Olsen?"

"Yes. Is that a problem?"

"My entire life, I've heard about the feud between our families. The Griffitts and the Olsens do not have anything to do with each other. I never knew why."

"I think the reason is standing right there between them. That's my great-great-grandmother."

Mack leaned closer too and peered at their faces. He could see the resemblance. It was his relative who gazed longingly upon the woman, but her arm was linked with Janie's family member. "Lost love. That explains it. You did go to school here?"

"Yes."

"I don't remember you. I'm sorry."

"I was known by a different name back then. Plain Jane. I remember you. You rescued me one time."

"I did?" He studied her face intently for a few moments, and for the life of him, he still could not recall her as a young woman.

"Several boys were barking at me, and you made them stop."

He was at a loss for words again, so he stared at her instead, his eyes lost in her gaze. Time stood still as a million possibilities ran through his mind when he looked at her face. He didn't want to leave her side.

"There you are. Hello, Mack." Deputy Jack appeared next to Janie, offered a hand to Mack, and placed an arm around her shoulders, which she gently shrugged off.

"I guess we should find our seats."

Janie turned to follow Jack, which didn't help to improve Mack's mood, and he wandered slowly to the front of the room to find the table tent with his name on it. He shook hands with Skip Olsen as he and his wife, Grace, took their seats at the head table on the opposite side of the podium. The crowd began to trickle in, the tables filled, and Mack sat there in a daze. The front table was reserved for the Olsen family, and he couldn't take his eyes off Janie. She, on the other hand, completely ignored him, never once looking his way. Instead, leaning her head closer to Jack as she listened to him talk. Wonder why he had been given a seat at the Olsen table?

Mack stabbed his steak with a fork in annoyance and began cutting off bites with his knife.

Christy tapped the microphone several times, and her voice seemed to drone on and on. He blocked it out. She had mentioned that he would be on the program later, but for the life of him he couldn't remember what he was supposed to do or say. He could wing it and she would be furious, but what did it matter at this point? He just wanted to talk to Janie.

The steak was good, which he ate in silence and was about to take another bite of potatoes when Christy hissed at him. "Mack, you're supposed to do the welcome."

He stood behind the podium, uttered a few words of greeting and glad you're here, and then sat down. Christy shot him daggers and stood behind the podium to ask Skip Olsen to come forward.

"My great-grandfather stepped onto a ship as a twenty-year-old man to start a new life, never knowing where his talents might lie," Skip said. "He eventually made his way to the plains where he began to acquire land and raise beef. He donated the land for what was to become the city of Dixon."

Christy presented him with an award for the founding family. A wooden plaque with a gold plate and black text.

The Olsens
Founding Family
Est. 1917
For your vision, generosity, and perseverance in the development of Dixon, Texas.

Skip nodded and smiled while the crowd applauded, and then he stepped up to the microphone again. "My daughter, Janie, would like to say a few words."

Mack froze as Janie stood and walked his way. He felt as though he were in a trance and that they were the only ones in the room. He wondered if she might be a little nervous about speaking, but instead, she seemed to exude a confidence, maybe learned in the military.

"Thank you, everyone. I've had the opportunity recently to do some research, and I'd like to share with you what I've discovered.

"The Griffitt family was also one of the earliest settlers in this area. I believe it was Mack's great-great-grandfather who was our first postmaster, receiving mail at his dugout until his house was built. The Schulte family set up a tent close to where the bank is now and opened a barber shop. Cut and shave for a quarter. The Moore family's great-great-grandmother baked pies and cakes, eventually opening the first cafe. That's just a few, there are many others.

"These people had a vision of a community. They did not shun away from a hard day's work, and they made it possible for us to stand here today and celebrate their legacy. Congratulations to you all for continuing to be a part of Dixon."

The crowd applauded and Janie and Skip returned to their seats.

"We have coffee and a special cake, if Skip and Grace would like to cut the first slice," said Christy. "Please help yourself, stay, enjoy your dessert, and look at the photographs."

41

JANIE

BEFORE RETURNING TO HER TABLE, JANIE turned and faced Christy. "I just want you to know that you did an outstanding job on this event. Thank you so much for your hard work."

Christy looked at her with a stunned expression, and then she smiled. "I really appreciate you for saying that. I didn't know you had researched the families here."

"I love history," said Janie. "I was curious about the people who lived here before us, and after seeing the faces in those photographs, I appreciate the history even more. The display turned out to have quite an impact. You did an amazing job on this. Thank you, Christy."

"I like them as well. They'll hang in the chamber office after tonight." Then Christy said, "I think we might be able to be friends, Janie."

"I think that is a possibility. I hope so." There was so much more to be said between them, but neither one spoke again. Janie smiled at her before turning and walking to her table. She watched her father clutching the award and tried to fathom who the people were five generations before her. Were any of the women like her —resilient, independent, a little feisty. She chuckled to herself. But also, different. Were they all ranching people? Or did some march to their own beat? She looked around the table where she sat. Her brothers Nathan and Travis, their wives, and sister Angie, had all gathered around their father to admire the plaque. They were hard-working, proud people. It was too bad Libbie hadn't come home from college. Janie felt like she had lost touch with her youngest sister Libbie, but then she had gone through that phase as well, breaking away from home and family to be on her own. She thought that's what she had wanted, but at that very moment, she realized being back in Dixon wasn't near as bad a place as she thought when she had left.

Mack walked over to shake her father's hand. They had a chuckle about the Olsen and Griffitt family feud. While Mack talked, she stared at him. Definitely the most imposing man in the room, he had worn a dark suit with black cowboy boots, a starched white shirt and a bolo tie. Devilishly handsome. That's how she would describe him. And nothing remotely like anyone who would ever be interested in her.

"Can I bring you cake?" he suddenly turned from her father and looked at her.

For a moment, Janie was too stunned to answer. His steady gaze bore into her. The nearness of him caused her heart to jolt and her pulse to pound.

"Janie?" he said as he lightly touched her shoulder. "Cake?"

Before she could answer, Deputy Jack came hurrying towards them holding up his phone. "Did you get the notification? House fire."

Mack pulled his phone out of his pocket and Janie reached for hers on the table.

They each read the address and message: "House fire. Residents trapped inside."

Mack took hold of her arms. "I've got to go. You stay here."

And Janie said to herself, "I will not."

Various attendees at the award dinner, including Travis, received the same text on the county app. They rushed for the door.

Janie looked at Travis and nodded. "See you there."

Her mother tried to say something, but Janie was already out the door and running to her car.

42
MACK

As Mack's vehicle flew down the road, he punched a button on his cellphone for the dispatcher.

"Everyone notified? How bad is it? What about occupants?"

The 9-1-1 operator on the other end relayed scant details. It was all they had at this point.

"If they're on the county app, everyone's gotten the message. It's a two-story house. The 9-1-1 call said a few residents are unaccounted for. One is elderly. Others are children."

He hated to hear that. The memory of his father always haunted him when he answered a call, but he sensed his father and God were with him now.

"I'll be there in two minutes. Where's the engine?"

"Just ahead of you."

"Thanks. 10-4."

Mack steered his vehicle onto a farm road where there were sporadic houses. As he rounded a bend, he saw the bright red lights from the fire engine flashing over the structure and dry grass. Orange flames roared

230

from one end of the structure. This was a big one, and it was waging war.

A line of volunteers trailed behind him with flashers blinking.

He came to an abrupt stop a little away from the engine, jumped out, and put his bunker gear on, pants, jacket, gloves, and helmet, blending in with the other firefighters who wore the same uniform. Right away, he gave instructions.

"Get a headcount. What residents were in the house? Is anyone missing? Be careful with that hose until everyone's out. We don't want the roof caving in on them."

The sound of windows breaking disturbed Mack. It could mean compartment fires where one room of the house is hotter than another. Orange flames and smoke leaped out of two windows. One side of the roof suddenly ignited.

Some firefighters had gained access to the residence where the fire had not reached yet. Sounds of crashing could be heard. Axes against walls to release the heat. Men called out for residents to identify themselves, if they were still in the building.

He saw that the front door was open and the area was not engulfed. Yet.

"Get over to the door! Is that someone coming out? Get over to them."

Smoke was billowing everywhere.

Mack stared at the front door through his cloudy face mask. He couldn't get his father out of his mind. *Please, God, let someone come out.*

Suddenly, an older woman in a nightgown and robe, bedraggled hair, stumbled out. Her hands pushed a child on each of her sides ahead of her and out the door. The trio stumbled in coughing fits, and the firefighters and medical personnel rushed in.

Mack was so relieved. For the first time since he left the awards dinner, he could breathe a little slower. Hopefully, he'd see Janie later tonight. Or else, in the morning. Gosh, he wanted to talk with her so badly.

"Chief, it's a grandmother and two kids."

"Great," he said. "Good work."

The firefighter stared at him. "They say one more kid is upstairs. Hasn't come out yet. Went to find the dog. It was a cousins' slumber party."

A cold chill ran up his back.

"We've got to find that kid!"

As Mack turned to instruct other men on a strategy, he heard a woman's anxious voice as a swirling vision of red appeared out of the corner of his eye. He spun around to see Janie quizzing one of the firefighters. "What's the family's name?"

The firefighter looked at his clipboard. "The grandmother said it's La Barinda."

"That's Linda from the race! The girl who fell with me."

Mack grabbed her by the arms and yelled. "What are you doing here? I told you to stay back at the dinner."

"Is anyone going in? You've got to hurry and get her out."

"Janie, we are evaluating the situation. You're not helping any by getting in our way and wasting our time. Please get back in your vehicle."

"While you're evaluating, Linda is trapped upstairs! She might be hurt."

The cell phone of the firefighter at his side rang off. The man held it to his ear and looked at Mack. "It's the dispatcher. He got a call from the girl's mother. Frantic.

Wants to know if the girl is okay. Did she come out with the grandmother?"

Another firefighter dropped to the ground in a coughing fit. Other guys treated him with oxygen and water.

Mack surveyed the busy scene. Trucks, flashing lights, and men scurried about. He had to know how many people were in that house.

43
JANIE

JANIE WENT BACK TO HER VEHICLE AS MACK suggested. No, he ordered her.

Luckily, no one could see her since she had parked behind other volunteers. Trucks and vehicles had prevented her from parking too close.

At her car, she pulled out the heavy firefighter coat that Mack had given her. She crammed her helmet on, grabbed her gloves, and ran.

The horror of Linda trapped in that burning house chilled her to the bone. She had to get to that poor girl. She must be scared out of her mind.

"What are you doing?"

A voice behind her nearly gave her a heart attack.

"Oh, my gosh, Travis, you scared me." Janie glanced over her shoulder.

His face was serious, angry. He looked older than his years in the fireman's suit as he hurried after her. She didn't slow down.

"I asked what you're doing."

"Travis, help me. We've got to get that girl out. She's

upstairs. The girl from the race. Linda. Please."

"Chief ordered us all to stand down. It's too dangerous to go inside."

"What? He's giving up? If we don't go in, she'll die, Travis." She stopped and turned to face him. "I am going in with or without you."

He sighed. "Can't believe I'm saying this. What's your plan?"

"The back door. If you just get me in, I promise I can get to the second floor."

"You're crazy, you don't know the damage inside."

"The fire is burning at the opposite end of the house. I can get in through the back door. I have to try. The big engine is in the front near Mack. The small tanker truck is on the side. They're not using that hose. Some of the guys from the tanker have gone around to the front. Grab an ax, meet me at the back. If I need it, can you use the tanker hose?"

"Sure." He looked at his sister. "Janie? Say a prayer. I don't want anyone gettin' hurt in this thing. Mom'll have my hide."

"Will do, Travis. Don't worry. We'll be fine. Let's just get Linda out."

They walked around bushes to the back of the house. Travis peeked inside the tanker truck and saw keys in the ignition. If need be, he would be able to move the truck closer.

Helmet and face mask in place, Janie clicked on the regulator so she'd have air inside the building. She and Travis exchanged fist bumps. She gave a thumbs up and went through the back door.

Immediately she was engulfed in smoke. The jacket was heavy, as were the boots and the air compressor on her back. She carried a Halligan tool which would come in handy for prying something open or breaking something down. Testing the walls with the silver tool, she felt around to the stairwell. It was still intact, thank God. She raised the face shield and hollered up the stairs, "Linda! Are you up there? It's Janie!"

A coughing fit overtook her, so she crouched lower and eased up the stairs to the second level.

No answer. She'd have to go up. She had no choice.

A couple of rooms on the first floor were full of smoke, but the flames seemed to be contained on the second floor. The staircase should be intact and safe for her to walk on. She could see the flickering red lights from outside the windows through the fog and hear the crew's voices. Water pounded on the roof and sides of the structure as the firefighters directed their hoses.

Heading for the stairs, Janie tested each step with the Halligan. Halfway up, her radio crackled, but no voice sounded. She had told Travis to maintain radio silence so Mack wouldn't be on to them. One of the steps squeaked. Maybe because it was an old house. Or maybe because it was about to fall down. She hurried to the top and looked right, then left. Which way? *Help me, God.*

A faint sound. Was that a whine? A dog?

"Linda! Linda, are you here? It's Janie from the race. Call out."

She went to the door on the left, felt with her tool, then quickly removed her glove. It was hot. She rapped with the tool. "Linda! You in there?" No answer.

A crashing sound below. Wooden beams falling from the ceiling.

She stood in front of the bedroom on the right. And heard the low whining dog again.

"Linda! Linda!" She banged on the door, then touched

it. A little warm but not blasting hot. Smoke was seeping out from under the door.

She had to take the chance. Slowly she turned the knob and pushed the door open.

The room was full of smoke.

She remembered her training. Should she bust that window and let the smoke out?

She dropped to the floor and felt around, constantly calling Linda's name, but her voice was muffled behind the helmet shield. She also added, "Here, doggie. C'mere, boy." And then a kissy sound. Although that was difficult, and she coughed. And felt lightheaded.

As she was inching her way through the room towards the window, she thought she saw something move, but it was quick. Was it a tail fluttering or a little animal body scampering out of her way? More whining.

"Ow." She tripped over something and fell to her knees, the knees she had scraped in the 5K race. Man, that hurt. Feeling around on the floor, she felt something soft. A body.

She jostled what felt like a leg. "Linda! Is that you? Wake up!"

Moans came from the girl. And then low growls from the canine. Oh, great. "It's okay, poochie. I'm only here to help."

She shook Linda. "Wake up, Linda! We have to go."

It was only a couple of feet away. She took the Halligan with two hands like a spear and poked the window hard, then ducked to the side. Smoke plumed out and glass shards fell to the floor. "We're up here!" Janie screamed as loud as she could.

The dog gave a big bark. More like a yip.

"Janie? Is that you?" The girl said, coughing.

She could hear Travis yelling. "They're up here! Over here, guys!"

Janie crawled back. "Linda, how are you? We should be able to see and breathe a bit better with that smoke out of here soon. But looks like more is coming from the door. I'm going to give you some oxygen, but we'll have to share. I'm not supposed to take my mask off."

She could see the girl clearer now that the smoke was moving. And she saw a little white dog. Hopefully, it wouldn't bite her.

The most important thing was to get them to safety. Should she wait for a ladder, or chance going back down the stairs?

"Linda, focus. Stay awake. We have to get to that window. Is this your dog?"

"Yes. This is Snookums. I had to come back for him."

"Okay, hold onto him so we don't have to hunt him down."

She pressed the button on her helmet mic. "Mayday, mayday. We're upstairs in a back bedroom. Not sure we can make it down the stairs."

A frantic voice came on the speaker. "Janie! Is that you? Are you in the house?"

"Yes, Mack. I've got Linda and the dog. She's been hit on the head. I broke a window. Can we get the engine's ladder up to it?"

"You're surrounded by fire. We were just about to hit the roof with more water. Stay where you are. Away from the door. We'll move the engine closer. Move to the window if you can."

"I'm sorry, Mack. I just had to get her."

"Hold on, Janie. We're coming for you."

Janie tugged on Linda's arm as they crawled closer to the window and then alternated oxygen with the girl by taking turns with her face mask. Linda held tight to the little dog.

Smoke was filling the room again when Janie heard the ladder knock against the window frame. A boot and a leg of one of the firefighters emerged into the room, his arms reaching for them. Janie guided Linda towards him and handed him the dog, which he stuffed inside his jacket. They lifted Linda onto the ladder, and he carefully guided the girl down the rungs. Janie perched on the windowsill, relief washing over her as she watched him slowly help the girl down each rung. Linda jumped to the grass.

"You're next, Janie." She could see Travis standing at the bottom of the ladder. She was suddenly out of air and exhausted. Her eyes closed, and instead of swinging out and putting a foot on the top ladder rung, she toppled back into the room.

"Janie!"

She knew that voice.

"Janie, let's get you out of here. Stand up! I'll be with you every step of the way."

"Mack." Her voice was faint. She breathed his name, not even sure if she had said it aloud. She wanted desperately to go to that voice.

She felt a firm grip on her arm. As she swung a leg out of the window, Mack helped her onto the ladder. They were drenched within seconds.

"Keep those hoses on them, guys!"

The voices and shouts were below, faint as if she were in a well.

Mack held her tight the whole way, taking steps together, carefully. Another firefighter waited below them on the ladder just in case Mack needed help. It was her brother, Travis.

Finally at the bottom. Janie's legs were like jelly and she collapsed to the ground, Mack's arms still surrounding her.

"Get the ambulance over here! Now!" he yelled. After removing her helmet, gloves, and jacket, he gently placed his face next to hers. "Please don't leave me, Janie."

Travis got close too, face to face, their noses almost touching. "Janie! Stay with us."

Mack looked up, tears forming in his eyes, shaking his head. "She's going to be okay. She has to be okay."

"I'll call my folks." Travis disappeared.

Janie wanted to stop her brother. No reason to worry her parents. She was good. I'm fine. And then her world went black.

44
MACK

THE AIR AMBULANCE WAS ON SITE WITHIN minutes and left with the little girl, Linda. Helicopter blades chopping the night sky, sirens screeching, red lights flashing. The dog was safely in the care of the grandmother, and along with the other two children, everyone was okay. Mack's body shook, and he took shallow breaths as he climbed into an ambulance, ducking and folding his body onto a narrow bench. He leaned over Janie, still unconscious. He wasn't usually a praying man, but this time he knew the situation was not under his control. The only will that would prevail was God's. He knew the feeling of having a burning inferno rip someone you cared about out of your life forever.

The back door closed with a clank and someone banged on the vehicle. They were on the move, slowly navigating the streets of the neighborhood under the shrill pitch of the siren and heading for the open highway.

Please don't take her from me.

Janie's eyes were closed, the oxygen mask firmly on her face. She looked so small and helpless, like a small child on that gurney. He tried not to squeeze her hand too tightly. A paramedic was at her head pumping fluids and tracking vitals.

"How's her pressure?" Mack asked.

"Elevated. But under the circumstances, not too bad. How is yours?"

Mack looked up. "I'm fine."

"Your hands are shaking."

"I'm just worried."

"You should get checked out at the hospital. You were in that building too."

"Not as long as she was."

He couldn't take his eyes off her. *Dear God, be with us.*

Her eyes fluttered, she lifted the oxygen mask to talk, her mouth moved, but no sounds came out. She found her voice, cracked and broken. "Mack? Is Linda okay?"

He wanted to yell at her and throw something, and then yell some more. Another part of him wanted to kiss her and never let her out of his sight ever again. He leaned closer to her face. "Yes, she's going to be okay. They're taking Linda to the hospital. How do you feel?"

She coughed. "I'm all right. Tired."

"You know, Janie, you shouldn't have been in that house. You disobeyed my order."

"You're not going to yell at me now, are you?" She chuckled, then coughed.

"No, I'll wait until tomorrow to yell. I'm just saying you're an ornery woman sometimes." He tried to return the mask on her face but she stopped him.

"Last I checked, I don't work for you."

"Yes, that's true. But you can't run into dangerous situations when someone tells you to stay clear. It's my fire scene. Seems like we've had this conversation before." Suddenly, beyond his control, he pictured the worst-case scenario and gulped in an involuntary sob. "Please don't ever do that again, Janie. I couldn't stand it if something happened to you."

He buried his head in her neck and she stroked his dark hair. "Oh, Mack. You're just a big teddy bear, aren't you? I knew you were all bark."

"Promise me?"

"Promise you what?"

"Promise me you'll never do anything like that again."

She hesitated. "I'll think about it."

Her eyes were fully open now, dark smudges covered her face, and she tried to sit up a little although he moved her back down.

Sadness clouded her eyes and she looked away. "That was some Founders' Day, wasn't it? And then the fire. Maybe you should give Christy a call. Let her know you're all right."

"We broke up."

Choking, she said, "You what?"

He covered her face with the oxygen mask, and she took several deep breaths before he continued. "We had a talk."

She pushed his hand and the mask away. "I'm sorry to hear that," she murmured, and then a big grin spread across her face. "Did she give you a reason?"

"Yeah. I don't look at her the way I look at you. She asked if I had a thing for you."

Janie smiled. "What did you tell her?"

"I said I did."

"Really? What kind of a thing?"

"The kind of a thing that says I'd like to kiss you right

about now. But you probably should have the oxygen mask back on, and we've got this paramedic sitting right next to us."

"Well, don't let that stop you, Chief. Aren't you in charge?" She grinned.

"Technically, no, not in this ambulance."

The paramedic smiled. "You're not bothering me. Just make sure you let her breathe some more, Chief."

His lips connected with hers for a moment, and it was the best feeling in the world. He had waited all day for that. His whole life, in fact.

He smiled. "Janie, there's something else I want to talk to you about. Something I want you to promise."

"This is a lot of promising. What is it, Mack?" She was still teasing him.

"Promise you'll never leave me." He was serious.

"What are you saying?"

"At the moment I almost lost you, I realized that I care deeply for you, Janie."

"Anything else?"

"You're gonna make me say it, aren't you?"

She laughed. "Well, yeah! You think you're gonna get off easy? I'm not easy, Mack."

"That's an understatement. You are not an easy woman. But I wouldn't have you any other way."

"So, what are we talking about?"

"Janie, for Pete's sake! I love you and I want to marry you! Spend the rest of my life with you. Grow old together. Have kids. I think I loved you the moment you knew the make and model of my Harley."

She laughed.

"What do you say? Will you be my wife?"

She smiled. She looked at the paramedic, who was also smiling. She asked him, "Is he on one knee?"

"Sort of," the guy looked at Mack's legs. "It's kind of hard in this small space. Your oxygen saturation is up, and you're doing better, Janie. I think you're in the right mind to give him an answer."

"I'm doing much better, thank you." She looked intensely into Mack's eyes. "I don't have any plans. I came home trying to find myself, and I found you instead." Mack kissed her again.

Her eyebrows raised inquiringly. "Do you have a ring?"

"Good grief, Janie! No, not yet. I'll get you one. A big old diamond. Wait a minute." He opened a drawer close to him, where they kept the bandages and tape, and pulled out a small, bright purple, thick rubber band. He took hold of her ring finger and wound the rubber band twice around it. "There, to match your do-rag. What do you say? Yes, or no?"

Janie reached up to her face and moved the oxygen mask in place to take several more breaths, took it off again, and then she looked right at Mack, a deep frown creased her forehead. "I came back home with the intention of only staying a few weeks, a month tops, and then I met you. Now I can't think straight. I have no idea what to do because I can't see a future without you in it. My future lies wherever you are. Wherever life takes us, I'll be at your side."

"What are you trying to tell me?" His heart beating wildly. He recognized the love in her eyes, and realized that was the look he had been searching for all his life.

"Yes, I'll marry you." She laughed.

He kissed her again, her lips warm and sweet, and then yelled his excitement. "Woo hoo!"

They rolled to a stop under the emergency room awning.

Crouching over, he stuck his head out the back of the ambulance. "We're getting married!"

The hospital attendants smiled as they helped to lower Janie's gurney and roll it inside.

"You're the one who's always cool and calm. What's got into you?"

He gripped her hand tightly as they rolled down the hall. "I have a reason to be happy. You make me happy."

Within the confines of the curtained exam room, they were finally alone.

"I love you with all my heart, with all my being." She tried to stand, so he helped her and their lips met again. Even more sweet and tender than before. After a few seconds, they came up for air. "Oh, and Mack... I'm not really a big diamond ring kind of girl. Now, if it's a Harley you're talkin' about, well, that's a whole 'nother thing."

"I'm still gettin' you a ring."

"Is this going to be a problem? You telling me what I like and don't like. Bossing me around?"

He shrugged.

She cupped his face in both hands. "Mack, *you* mean a great deal to me. And *you* forever will. I love you with all my heart."

"I love you, Janie."

"I love you too, Mack. But we really should discuss the organization of your supplies in the firehouse. It could be so much more efficient in how the guys stow their gear."

Mack couldn't wipe the silly grin off his face. "Will you promise me one more thing?"

Janie rolled her eyes up to the ceiling. "What now?"

"Will you ask your sister if you can keep that red dress?"

45
CHIMMI

THREE DAYS LATER

CHIMMI HAD WASHED AND WAS NOW ROLLING Miss Hattie's short, gray hair in tight little curlers. It has been the elderly woman's style for the past fifty years. Chimmi had been her hairdresser for at least ten of those years and was never successful in introducing Miss Hattie to a new hairdo. That was okay. Everyone who came to the Curl Up & Dye beauty shop enjoyed their visits and even made lifelong friendships.

The front door buzzed and in walked Belinda, carrying boxes of sweet baked goods from her coffee shop, the B&R Beanery. Kolaches—blueberry, apricot, or cream cheese inside. Some people might call them Danishes, but these were not those. Yummy, buttery, melt-in-your-mouth heavenly treats.

"Got the coffee on, Chimmi? Or tea."

"What's the celebration, Belinda?"

"I think you'll find out soon enough," she said behind a sly smile.

The ladies sat back, enjoying their coffees and sweet pastries.

Breaking their reverie, the door buzzed and in walked Janie with Angie on her heels.

"Good morning, girls! To what do we owe your visit?" Chimmi loved playing the welcoming hostess.

Angie strode in confidently and a bit loud as usual. She held her hand out towards Janie like Vanna White displaying the letters. "Well, it appears my big sister is gettin' hitched. I guess y'all probably know that by now. News spreads fast in Dixon."

Cheers and clapping erupted around the room.

"Yay, Janie!"

"He's very handsome," Miss Hattie commented.

"Handsome? He's hot!" one lady said.

Janie's face turned varying shades of pink, then the color traveled down her neck.

"I had hoped she could show you her ring, but it seems they've been a little busy to shop for it just yet. Being heroes and all that. Rescuing people from fires, then having a near-death experience herself." Angie glared at her sister but put an arm around Janie's shoulder.

"Oh, Janie, we're all so glad you weren't hurt in that fire." Chimmi went over to hug her. "And you have plenty of time to find the perfect ring."

"Well... uh, uh..." Janie was about to speak, but as usual, Angie jumped in.

Grabbing Janie's hand to extend it towards the room, she said, "In the meantime, she's wearing this double-wound rubber band that Mack found in the ambulance. Ain't that sweet?"

Now the room filled with collective "Awwws."

"You know, Janie," Chimmi started, "we all just knew that you and Mack would get together."

"How'd you know that?" Janie's head tilted to one

side as she helped herself to a kolache. "I didn't even know that."

All at once, different comments arose from the ladies from under the hair dryers and the manicure station.

"At the livestock show when you were supposed to help hand out awards..."

"At the Fourth of July parade..."

"When you rode on the back of his motorcycle to the canyon..."

"And on that double date when Jack left you stranded." The mention of that one caused the room to erupt into laughter.

Angie's smile was nearly as big as the sixty-foot cowboy on the Big Texan Steakhouse sign. "Did y'all do some matchmaking or something? Pretty tricky. But I approve. Janie needed help, and she sure wouldn't listen to me."

Janie's eyes widened and she looked from one lady to the next.

"Oh, I hope you're not mad at us." Chimmi touched Janie's elbow. "We only wanted the best for you and Mack. We could see you were meant for each other right from the start. And we were all praying for you, too."

"I'm not mad." Janie cleared her throat. "I'm gonna think of all of you as my guardian angels. Besides, I'm in love, so I can't be mad at anyone."

Angie laughed loudly. "I think she's also saying, 'Don't do it again.' Don't start naming their babies."

Janie turned towards her and halfway glared. "Easy. We're not in any hurry."

Karmelle stood and came towards them. "Janie, when you find the perfect ring, you come back and the manicure is on me."

"That's so kind. Thank you very much."

The others in the shop asked various questions.

"Where will you get married?"

"Where will you live?"

Janie looked from one to the other, trying to keep up.

"Maybe at the firehouse. And about the ring, Mack mentioned possibly giving me his grandmother's ring."

More oohs and ahs filled the room.

In all seriousness, Chimmi looked at Angie and Janie. "Shhh, don't ever tell our secret. We are a confidential group. Wouldn't want to have to kill ya." Chimmi winked.

"Okay. I know we took a blood oath. Or was it a grape juice oath?" Belinda giggled.

"Since I was your latest victim, seems only fair that I can join you." Janie looked at each of the ladies.

Karmelle was at the nail station getting ready for her next client. "Maybe we could have a secret sign. Like, however we get our nails painted—pink, French, whatever—we add an extra color, like purple, to just one pinky nail. We ALL get that special color on one nail. That would identify us as being a part of the secret Curl Up & Dye group. If anyone asks about it, we never tell." She was as excited as she had been as a young girl, pricking her finger with another little girl and mixing the liquid to establish them as blood sisters.

"You might be getting a little carried away, Karmy," her older sister said.

"I thought we weren't going to use those nicknames, Chi Chi." She shrugged.

"Just have a kolache and coffee and relax."

Belinda lifted her coffee in the air. "We really should have a toast, shouldn't we? Chimmi, will you please do the honors?"

"All right." She lifted her coffee too. "Here's to true

love. Mack and Janie. They might not have gotten together if it hadn't been for the ladies in this room. Some might call it meddling. But my mama would have called it looking out for others. Playing Cupid, so to speak. There's no harm in that. We didn't hurt anyone."

"To true love," all the ladies said, raising their drinks and following with cheers.

"What's our next order of business?" one of the ladies under the dryer asked.

"Well, before we get to that," Chimmi started, "...and I do have someone in mind... but don't you think we oughta first talk about the wedding? At the church on Main Street? Or at the firehouse?"

"Ooh, I know just the thing." Karmelle's face took on the look of having just ingested a sweet treat, which she did as she bit into a kolache, but she was conjuring up something altogether different in her mind. "Those young firefighters all lined up in their dark blue uniforms. Do they have uniforms? Or just T-shirts? Fire engines with ladders raised up and crossed. The bride and groom walking beneath the ladders. Wouldn't that be so romantic?" She let out a big sigh.

Belinda stared at her. "You have *got* to get out more. You've been watching way too many *Hallmark* movies."

All the ladies in the room cackled. One of them said, "I *love* Hallmark movies."

"We haven't really decided where the wedding will be." Of course, Janie's comments went unheeded. The conversation continued.

"Maybe Janie would like to get married at the Rafter O."

"No way. Remember her brother Travis was married there? And then his brand-new wife had a baby at the wedding reception!"

All the ladies started talking at once, sharing stories of where they were married.

Miss Hattie spoke up. "I married my husband, Henry, God rest his soul, sixty years ago in the church right on Main. It's always best to be married in a church, I always say, not in the driveway or garage of a firehouse." She grimaced.

Chimmi gently patted the older woman's shoulder. "I'm sure it was lovely, Miss Hattie. Let's get you under the dryer now, all right?"

"I've got it!" Karmelle blurted out. "On Harleys! With biker people invited. I betcha you would love that, wouldn't you, Janie? Afterwards, you can ride off into the sunset. With little 'Just Married' signs on the bumpers of your motorcycles. Wouldn't that be cool?"

Chimmi looked at Belinda. "I do believe my sister is coming out of her shell more and more these days. She is not the same mousy woman she was when she first moved here. And especially since she let me put those blonde highlights in her hair." To Karmelle, she smiled and said, "You wild woman, you."

"Mousy? I resent that. And I call them angel kisses in my hair. I am not wild. I am still a church-going lady."

They all giggled and pointed to Karmelle's tie-dye leggings.

"What? What are y'all lookin' at? These are comfortable for work."

"They are wild."

The room filled with laughter.

Chimmi waited for the chatter to settle and for Janie and Angie to leave before she made her big announcement. She clapped her hands. "Okay, ladies, settle down. I want to tell you about our next 'victim', although we really need a different word. How about lonely, lovesick, single? C'mon, help me here."

"Lookin' for Love. LFL."

"In all the wrong places."

More laughter filled the room.

"Just one word. How 'bout just 'lovesick'?"

"No, it's gotta be a name. Like we had 'victim'. Think like spies. Maybe 'target' or 'mark'."

Clapping her hands again, Chimmi said, "Let's just move on. We'll come up with a new name later. But for now... drum roll please... our next victim will be none other than Christy!"

Miss Hattie grumbled. "Christy at the chamber? But she was such a pill on our last case."

"C'mon, be nice. I saw Christy the other day at the market. She looked a little down. Then when I spoke to her, she acted all upbeat, like she's totally fine. She must have some hurt feelings if she had hoped it would've turned into more with him. It's sad being alone." Belinda was always the sympathetic one.

"I think I might know who she could get attached to."

"Do tell." Chimmi looked at her sister.

"I saw her flirting with Deputy Jack. And yes, I'd definitely call it flirting. On both their parts," Karmelle offered.

"Do you think he's high enough on the ladder for her? You know she always talks about a man of top standing."

"I heard Jack might run for sheriff. That's pretty high up in this town. He mentioned it to Russell the other day when he stopped by the coffee shop."

"If she manages his campaign, he'd be sure to win."

"I think Christy would make a really good mayor." A few gasps, and then all heads turned to Karmelle.

"What? She would. Leadership and organizational skills, politicking. She'd be good at it."

"We've never influenced a mayoral election before. But I agree. She'd be better than the one we've got now."

The wheels had started to turn. The town of Dixon would be in good hands. Even if it was happening behind the scenes.

Chimmi surveyed the occupants of the Curl Up & Dye. Her shop. She knew her husband would be proud of her. She was proud. Of herself. The ladies. Her town. This was family. Quirky maybe, but family nonetheless.

And Janie and Mack? Perhaps an unlikely pair at first. But Chimmi knew true love came in a variety of packages, some pretty hard to recognize. And it was never too late for love to come knocking on one's door. Chimmi wanted to help more people find it. And she'd be listening for herself and Karmelle, too. Even if the knock was a faint tap.

ACKNOWLEDGMENTS

Writing these books is a privilege and a joy, and we hope that readers will enjoy the stories and feel God's touch upon their lives. Many thanks to my co-author and dear friend, Natalie Bright; the Western Writers of America; Wolfpack Publishing and CKN Christian Publishing; and so many others who support our efforts.

~Denise F. McAllister

Thanks to my co-author Denise for her willingness to tackle another series. Thanks to Randy Griffitt, former Fire Chief of the Dimmitt Fire Department, my home-town, for his expertise on fire procedures and small-town fire departments, and thanks to Tami Griffitt for filling in the gaps on the details and people of our beloved home-town of Dimmitt, Texas. Special thanks to Carol Drew for sharing information and details of her husband Duane's forty-five years of service with the San Angelo Fire Department. Thanks to my brother-in-law, Randy Bright, for sharing his knowledge about all things Harley-Davidson. As always, thanks to my husband, Chris, for his support and encouragement.

~Natalie Bright

A LOOK AT: BOOK THREE

FINDING MY DESTYNEE

True heart's desire cannot be ignored...

Destynee Olsen has always done everything her mother asked, without argument. But she never realized that the road to stardom might mean leaving behind a piece of her heart.

Beginning to question whose dream she's really following, Destynee stumbles upon the power of gospel music and how she feels when she sings it. Wondering if it might be her true calling—rather than the Nashville country music scene that's grounded on her mother's lifelong dream—she wrestles with what she wants for her future.

Back home—and raising their only son—Travis Olsen is trying desperately to hold on to his vow to never stand in the way of Destynee's vision. But her path to stardom, as wondrous as it is, is slowly building in him feelings of resentment. And while there is no question that his wife has an unbelievable talent, he can no long stomach watching their son grow up without a mother.

Following the story of a woman whose mother said her destiny is much more important than she is, and a cowboy who refuses to upend his wife's lifelong dream, Destynee and Travis will have to figure out what's more important—their aspirations...or true heart's desire.

AVAILABLE OCTOBER 2022

ABOUT NATALIE BRIGHT

With roots firmly planted in the Texas Panhandle, Natalie Bright grew up obsessed with the Wild West and making up stories. The small farming community where she lived gave her a belief in hard-working, genuine people and a firm foundation of faith. She is the author of books for kids and adults, as well as numerous articles.

This author and blogger writes about small town heroes with complicated pasts and can-do attitudes, who navigate life's crazy misfortunes with humor and happy endings.

ABOUT DENISE F. MCALLISTER

Lovers of the West can be born in the most unlikely of places. For Denise F. McAllister, her start was in Miami, Florida, surrounded by beaches and the Everglades.

But the marvels of television transported her to stories of the West—*Bonanza, Gunsmoke, The Virginian, Big Valley, The Lone Ranger, Daniel Boone,* and many others— that she fondly recalls watching with her brother every Saturday morning.

After being in the working world for some years, Denise decided to apply her life experience and study for her B.A. in communications and M.A. in professional writing.

To this day, her faith is important to her, and she loves to write about characters' journeys as they navigate real-world challenges. She prays that readers will enjoy her books, but—more importantly—experience a blessed connection with their Creator and Heavenly Father.